ALL IS WELL

ALL IS WELL

Katherine Walker

Thistledown
Press

Thistledown Press Ltd.
P.O. Box 30105 Westview
Saskatoon, SK S7L 7M6
www.thistledownpress.com

Library and Archives Canada Cataloguing in Publication
Title: All is well / Katherine Walker.
Names: Walker, Katherine (Author of All is well), author.
Identifiers: Canadiana 20210186089 | ISBN 9781771872157 (softcover)
Classification: LCC PS8645.A46185 A75 2021 | DDC C813/.6—dc23

Cover and book design by Tania Craan
Printed and bound in Canada

Thistledown Press gratefully acknowledges the financial assistance of
The Canada Council for the Arts, SK Arts, and the government of Canada
for its publishing program.

For Jean

TERRY IS LYING on his back on the plush rug in the church office. The rug has a Garden of Eden motif. Terry's chin is jutting awkwardly away from the tree of knowledge, with its red, low-hanging fruit. If Christine could adjust his head, that would be better. With some minor corrections, Terry's airway would be clear.

The Reverend Christine Wright is filled with an urge to go to Terry there on the floor. To make sure he is still breathing and provide first aid. But no, Terry doesn't need a clear airway anymore, because Terry is dead.

It started when Terry lunged at Christine with his hands stretched out to seize her neck. In one movement, Christine grabbed the closest object and hit him with it—hard. The sound at impact was half thud, half crack.

Right before she hit him, the look on his face changed. She wasn't sure what she saw. Recognition? Resignation? This caused a small hiccup in the signal to her arm, but her arm carried through anyway. Candlestick-on-bone remains fat in her ears while her body absorbs the vibration.

The office, with its long, wooden vestry dressers and tall, full bookshelves, is quiet, as if in expectation. Christine steps around his body, lying so still in the middle of the thick, ornate rug. What is the look on his face now? His eyes are wide open and empty. No sign of recognition or resignation now. No sign of anything.

"Terry? Hey!" Weapon still in hand, Christine feels for his pulse, but there is nothing, just her own pulse in her fingers. She puts the heavy candlestick down on her desk and pulls her phone from her back pocket. Her thumb is shaking, but she unlocks the phone and is about to punch in 9-1-1. She is formulating what she'll say to the operator. Terry's age, nature of injury, location. The words candle-stick and library flash into her mind. She laughs—part choke, part gasp. She covers her mouth. Her hand smells like metal.

She shoves her phone back in her pocket. She needs to act before the adrenaline is gone.

The church is empty and locked. Before Terry showed up, Christine had just sent Mrs. Wilson home for the night. Mrs. Wilson is one of three people who had come for the service, and the only volunteer for the vigil. It is just after nine p.m. on Good Friday. Christine's first Easter as a priest.

She reaches for the switch by the back door and kills the office lights. She steps onto the couch where Terry had sat, making a confession to her, or whatever that was.

She had known when he walked in the door that something wasn't right. He looked extra wolfish. He moved too close, too fast.

Wobbling a bit on the soft couch seat, she peers out the win-dow. Past the graveyard, she can see the front entrance of the church hall, where the Friday night Alcoholics Anonymous meet-ing is just letting out. Christine wonders who might have seen Terry come to the office, which serves also as the vestry, at the back of the church.

There's a back door from the office that leads to the grounds-keeper's shed, a few parking spaces, and the residence where she now lives. The residence is to the east and the church hall to the west, with the graveyard in between. All is reassuringly quiet, except for the AA folks, who are laughing and hugging one another goodnight.

Ron, a silver-haired AA old-timer with a pompadour like Elvis, keeps looking over at her back door. She watches him sweep up cigarette butts, turn out lights, and lock up. Christine ducks below the windowsill when Ron walks past to drop the garbage in the dumpster by the shed. She hears his nervous whistle as he makes his way along the side of the church and past some graves.

It's a beautiful churchyard, the way the graves are nestled in between the church and the hall, and how the graveyard opens up to gardens and the boundary along a regional park. They tried to send her somewhere nice. She's lucky to be here—or no, unlucky. But Terry's luck is worse than hers tonight.

What's Ron up to?

She hears him walk around the pile of building materials for the labyrinth and Larry's backhoe, which have been sitting beside the dumpster for months. Church Council is putting in a labyrinth off the main parking lot, in between the church and the church hall. Another last-ditch effort to attract more parishioners and keep the church from closing. A circular maze that you mindfully walk into, slowly searching out answers to questions. Why does my life suck? Why are people so horrible? Why did I just kill someone with a candlestick?

There are bricks, sand, and some topsoil piled up in the residence parking lot. The sand is adjacent to the grave of one Mr. Marshall. He died over eighty years ago. This is good—the ground around his grave already looks a bit disrupted.

Ron is taking his time finishing up. Christine can't make her move until he's gone.

Moments after Ron's car leaves, Christine lets herself into the shed. It's cool and smells of cedar. Mrs. Dee—the church's warden—and her minions keep the shed, like everything else in the parish, immaculate. Christine grabs a pair of gloves and a spade.

Christine looks up into the sky to ask forgiveness for what she is about to do. The moon is out and nearly full, and the gravestones look eerily beautiful. Impressed with the sharp, carbon-steel blade, Christine drives the tip into Mr. Marshall's peaceful resting place. Her adrenaline dwindled long ago. It doesn't matter, Christine can dig a trench in six minutes. All will be well.

Just before midnight, Christine is physically exhausted, and embarrassed that it has taken nearly three hours to dig a trench for Terry. It's too shallow, but Christine can't dig any more. Shaking with fatigue, she stumbles back to the office to get Terry.

She rolls Terry up in the rug, using two silken, braided cinctures to tie it as tight as possible. Christine stops herself from tying a dovetail on the end and catches herself murmuring the vesting prayer for the cincture: "Bind me, O Lord, with the cincture of purity, and quench in my loins any longings of lust, and that chastity and continence may always abide within." Once tied, she grabs the edge of the rug and tugs. He's damn heavy, too much for a fireman carry.

"Right. Let's go, Terry."

It takes a good five minutes to drag him—stopping every few yards to tighten up the rug so he doesn't spill out—to the damn hole. She has now kick-rolled Terry. Christine has no idea which way he is facing, but he's going to be just shy of two feet under. It's that damn rug. Bloody hell.

"Sorry, Terry."

Christine fills the shallow hole and levels out the hollows in the surface of the grave with shovelfuls borrowed from Larry's piles of dirt and sand. Now it looks like Larry's pile spilled a little onto the grave. Then she uses the spade to clumsily rake over her footprints.

Gloves and spade stowed in the shed, Christine returns to the office to lock it up. The office is temporarily cluttered from Maundy Thursday with the fonts, emptied of holy water, the liturgical vessels, all candles, and anything indicating the presence of Christ.

Maundy Thursday is about the betrayal of Jesus, and the darkness that brings. To enact this, she and Tom washed everyone's feet and then she read out the betrayal. Then, in total silence they extinguished the candles, stripped the altar of its linens, washed the bare altar, removed everything, shut off the lights and left the congregation to find their way out in the dark.

Tom, her server, an ex-tough guy, got the point and became a little alarmed with the rite. This is good. He's tough, but his earnest hunger for recovery, for redemption, softened that tough exterior. Maundy Thursday is disturbing, it's supposed to be. All the stuff will go back into the church tomorrow.

Christine sees the candlestick sitting on her desk. Holy hell. When she lifts it up, it leaves a ring of dark red on the wooden surface. The edge of her shoe is sticky with Terry's blood. First a shallow grave, and now this. Someone might think she's not very good at this kind of thing.

She locks the office door and heads back to the shed. Her muscles are quivering. She grabs two jugs of something with a corrosive symbol on it. This is stupid, so Christine also grabs a heavy-duty mask and thick, elbow-length gloves. Leaving the shed, she walks past the dumpsters, past her car to the residence, a tall, skinny Victorian, her home now. There is a driveway for the residence off busy Yates Street, and room for three or four cars along with the garbage dumpsters. The residence is pushed up against the park boundary, where the growth is thick. The place is almost totally private at the moment.

She stumbles in the dark, nearly dropping the chemicals. With barely any parishioners or money left, the grounds are no longer lit. Just one light in the main parking lot. Darkness is not normally an issue for Christine, or rough terrain, or carrying objects for that matter. She's Military, and she's seen action. Action is the nice word for extreme violence and death. Her handling of violence and death is now officially considered heroic, and she has a Victoria Cross hidden in her closet that proves it.

What's worse than getting people killed? Getting a medal for it. Especially that medal. She doesn't deserve it.

Thick and tall blackberry bushes, with their sharp thorns, mark the boundary between the parish grounds and the park. Beyond that, there are tall cedars, twisted arbutus, and firs that surround a deep freshwater lake.

Christine kicks her boots off at the front door and makes her way back to the kitchen, closing doors behind her. She opens all the windows in the kitchen. The white curtains billow, flap, and twist. In and out—as if the wind is breathing through the house. The weather has changed. It's stormy and about to rain.

She reads the label on the container, wondering what chemicals it contains and what they'll do to a candlestick. The words blur. She puts the plug in the sink, masks and gloves up, and pours both jugs into the same basin. No hissing or explosions—good enough. She holds the candlestick under the surface of the brown sludge like she's drowning the thing. Then she turns it over slowly, as the crud drips from it, checking for traces of blood. Nothing. She begins to scrub it with a nail brush, holding her face as far as possible from the caustic bath.

Her doorbell rings, and she jumps. She ferries the candlestick quickly over to her kitchen table and puts it down on a napkin, strips off the gloves and mask, and, closing the door behind her, walks down the hall to the front door landing.

Christine can see a dark shape through the heavy, bevelled glass in the door. It is Shawna, Terry's partner, with their infant child. It has started to rain. Shawna is inches from the door, under the narrow overhang.

Christine opens the door and steps into the doorway.

"Shawna. It's after two in the morning."

"Yeah, I know, Reverend."

The baby squirms in her carrier. Shawna pulls her rain hood back. Her waist-long mane of glamorous hair is pulled back into a ponytail. Her long, narrow face is contorted with worry.

"Can I come in?" Shawna moves before Christine does, pushing past her into the landing.

Christine would normally be putting the kettle on at this point or asking if she could heat up a bottle. Ordinarily, she would be putting some of Mrs. Dee's cookies on a plate. This time, Christine just stands there. Very still.

"What's going on, Shawna?"

"It's Terry. He didn't come home after the meeting. This isn't like him. Well, it is—but not tonight."

"So, when was the last time you saw him?"

"I just told you. Before the meeting." Shawna marches into the living room and sits down. She is expecting immediate service. Even in a ponytail, Shawna's long, shiny chestnut hair moves like a waterfall.

The lights are off. Shawna is sitting in the dark. Christine stays on the landing. The rain is pouring down, and she can see a semi-transparent reflection of herself in the lead glass pane in the door. She finds the line between her body and the darkness by moving. Her dark shape is pointed at the top, like a flame.

The baby is unhappy, and Shawna is rocking her in the carrier on the floor.

"Can I, uh … can I have a glass of water?"

"Of course." Christine opens the closet by the back door and pulls a bottle out of the dust-covered flat of bottled water on the lower shelf and hands it to Shawna, who unscrews the cap and drinks the bottle in several large gulps.

Now what, Christine wonders. "Do you want to pray?" she asks.

Shawna is quickly on her feet, carrier in arm, empty water bottle tossed onto the seat of the couch. "No, Reverend, you know I don't want to pray. I want to know where the fuck Terry is."

"Right." Christine says.

"He came here."

"He did?"

Shawna tosses her ponytail. "Yeah. He did."

Christine shrugs. "I didn't see him. What about the meeting? You said …"

The baby is cooing now, her large blue eyes slowly scanning the ceiling. Big blue eyes, just like Terry.

"That doesn't make sense."

"Did you call his sponsor?" Christine asks.

"No. Terry doesn't use him anyway."

"Hmm." Christine can barely stand upright. She is starting to shut down.

Shawna pushes. "I know he came here. I told him he had to, to see you. Confess. Get that thing out of him. Or I would leave. We would leave."

Christine is slumping into the wall. She brings one leg up as if to do a yoga tree pose, to try to stay awake on her feet. Suddenly, she half falls toward Shawna and the baby. She was too inactive through all the years of theological school. She's so out of shape, it's pathetic.

"I'm sorry, Reverend. It's late. Terry's just a real handful, you know? Tonight, things got super scary. We both said and did things."

Christine summons the last of her fading energy to stifle a laugh. "I understand. Listen, if he's not back in twenty-four hours, we'll report him missing, okay? I'm sure everything is fine."

Shawna reaches for the door handle. She looks down at Christine's shoes.

"Were you working in the graveyard?"

"No, no, not the graveyard. The labyrinth."

Feigning interest. "What's a labyrinth?" Shawna is outside, under the overhang. The rain is coming down hard now.

"It's a maze." Christine blinks. Her eyeballs are dry, gravelly.

"Do you have to find your way out?"

"In. Goodnight, Shawna, don't worry, sleep well."

"Wait, what do you mean *in*?" She looks directly at Christine, her expression open. "I mean, what's the point? Do you find something in the centre?"

"Sometimes."

"What?"

"God."

Christine closes the door and Shawna dashes to her car, holding her jacket over her child. Christine locks the door. Sometimes. Sometimes you find God. Because God's not always there.

A short time later, Christine is showered and kneeling beside her bed. Routine and discipline put her here. Last and first conscious moments—when possible. She has more of these moments now as a civilian. Waking up on operations usually doesn't afford much quiet time. Or sleep.

After the years piled up in the military, her body got used to moving on its own while her mind went over vital details. Christine reminds herself that she is out of the military now. That way of life is finished for her. Time to pray and get her head down. She'll go see Joey tomorrow. Joey will know what to do.

Christine forces her body to relax. This is one of the reasons she gets down on her knees to pray. It's hard to fight anything on your knees. AA taught her to keep it simple. Just say thank you at night and turn your will over to God in the morning. Christine gets ready to say thank you to the God that pulled her out of hell. As far as she can tell, anyway.

She can't do it. She's had some intense missions, but what happened tonight was new. Terry is—was—a civilian. And a candlestick—what the fuck? Is God toying with her? Is she out of hell or not? Maybe God should make up God's mind.

A freight train of justifications—he was going for her throat, he was stoned and crazy—rushes through her mind.

Enough. She grits her teeth. "Thank you. Thank you. Thank you," she says to the ceiling over her bed. To the God she hopes has her back.

HER DOORBELL GONGS. Once. Twice. Christine grabs her phone: 9:32. There's a text from Joey. He's responded to her plea for help.

"10:00am Too"

Too, Joey's favourite noodle house, is not far away. Joey had been assigned to her as a spiritual director by her bishop, to see her through to ordination, but Joey seems to know she still needs him. Christine puts on her robe and forces her stiff, cramping legs to hustle down the stairs as the doorbell rings again.

She opens the door to a dishevelled-looking Mrs. Dee—is her hair actually uncombed?—carrying a newspaper and a cookie tin.

"Reverend. Please understand that I'm reluctant to disturb your apparently subdued Saturday. But I'm afraid something absolutely horrible has happened. There's been a theft! The office rug has been stolen. I was about to call the police, but it's best if you call, don't you think?"

Mrs. Dee is already past her, and in the kitchen. Mrs. Dee, with her pillowy bosom and round, fleshy face, appears soft and tender, but looks can be deceiving. Mrs. Dee is like a nervous rabbit.

Christine is starving, her head is pounding, and there's this rabbit woman in her kitchen, nattering on about rugs. Mrs. Dee opens the cupboard where the cookies go, pulls out the old tin, and puts the new tin in. She's left the copy of the local paper, *Coastal Life*, on the table in the landing.

Christine shuffles into the kitchen and lowers herself gingerly into a chair at the table. Mrs. Dee faces her, holding the tin of last week's cookies.

"You didn't go through barely any. Do try to remember, I want you to use these. Shall I fetch the phone for you? We need to call the police. I'm not—" Mrs. Dee sees the candlestick and takes a step back, dropping the tin with a bang onto the floor. She picks up the candlestick with two hands, like it's an injured kitten.

"What ... what has happened here?" The candlestick is tarnished. Okay, so it's beyond tarnished—it's black. So what? Christine must not laugh. She picks up the old tin of cookies, opens the lid, and starts eating. The laughter wants to come. She needs to be careful not to choke.

"I brought it back with me last night."

"Do you think I cannot see that? That is quite evident to me, really. It is. I am, after all, holding it in my hand right now. But what have you done to it?"

"I had to clear the church afterwards, and, well, walk back here. It was so dark. So I brought the stick along. Not really sure." She speaks around the delicious oatmeal cookie she's just stuffed into her mouth.

Mrs. Dee starts looking like a face shifter. Like a chameleon. Like that Michael Jackson video, but not with the upbeat tune. Her faces are many, and they shift quickly. Anger, frustration, and scorn are this morning's blend. And anxiety. The anxious face is always there. That's a constant. Christine hopes Mrs. Dee's taken her heart meds. Christine doesn't have time for this.

She can't help Mrs. Dee calm down. What irks Mrs. Dee the most is that she has no way to control Christine. Christine is not employed by the parish, she is being paid by the military, so they get a priest for free. This is part of the reintegration program. Her reward for being a hero. So none of Mrs. Dee's threats involving the mighty Church council or those alluding to a paycheque will work.

"Do tell me how it is that you've come to call this precious gem of Christ's Church a stick? It is not a stick, I might add. And I don't bake those for you."

Christine closes the lid on the cookies. "I just thought—"

"I'll remind you again—do try to remember—they go to the shelter when unused here."

It's 9:45. Christine jumps up. You can't be late for Joey. That's his only rule. You're late—he's gone.

"Mrs. Dee, I have to go."

"What about the police? The rug!"

"I'll take care of it."

Christine leaves Mrs. Dee with her smashed old cookies and blackened stick. Fifteen minutes is fine. It's only a five-minute drive. She struggles into white dress pants and a white, long-sleeved blouse. After all, it's Saturday Vigil. This is the day everything crammed in the office will go back out into the church. Mrs. Dee and her minions will polish that stick and everything else. The altar, silver, wood, and windows will gleam. Christine should really be greeting and helping the people who do show up. Christine's duty as she understands it today is to feed that anticipatory Easter tension by being smiley and upbeat. She is supposed to be acting like polishing and cleaning a church will do something about the horrifying reality that is the human condition.

Not right now. She needs to see Joey. It's better this way because Christine's version of upbeat is not upbeat. Christine's version of upbeat is disturbing.

AS CHRISTINE PULLS her vehicle out onto the shady street, she notices that there are many people out, adorned in bright colours and moving with a purpose. Something big is happening downtown. Is it a festival, or a parade? Worse, it's a run. The Fun Run. Oh no, a run that literally encircles a part of downtown Victoria. People are out in a big way. This is the first Fun Run since the pandemic. Extra, super fun.

Stupid civilians. How they insist upon their fun. Not fun for the people who need an ambulance from inside the running loop on Fun Run day. Not fun for someone whose reintegration program is a disaster and who may now be facing a prison sentence for murder. Don't these fun runners get it? There's no fun to be had today. They need to get the fuck out of her way.

It's 9:54 by the time Christine sees that she can drive no further amid the throngs of people. Christine pulls into a parking spot that is miraculously free just before Vancouver Street, but some blocks from Too café.

Regretting her heels, she jogs to Vancouver Street, which is flagged off, expecting it to be free of people. Christine looks down to the right—she's two blocks down from the start line. The race doesn't start until ten a.m., and there are a whole bunch of firefighters, military, and other elite athletes warming up, looking grimly determined, not here for fun. These types must run five minutes before, to avoid any stampeding or ugliness. Because that's not fun.

Vancouver Street is lined with three-storey apartment buildings. The trees are large and high, and they bend over the street, providing a shady arch. The route winds through Beacon Hill Park, along Dallas Road, and crosses the finish line in the Inner Harbour, where yachts bob in front of the Empress Hotel.

The starter sounds, and here they come.

The flagged-off street fills with serious runners charging past her. Christine needs to fight her way across to get to Joey on time. It's just a two-lane street—how hard can it be? She used to sprint a mile and a half in nine minutes. Over hills, plural. Steep hills. And then sharpshoot. Accurately. And then swim in the ocean. She was Special Forces. This is a two-lane road. Easy. All will be well.

She steps into the street and starts running alongside a racer, who gives her a confused sideways glance. She cuts behind him over to the next runner. Easy. No problem. She's going to be on time. As she makes a few strides over to the next runner, a guy sheathed in blue spandex barrels into her and she falls hard onto the pavement.

Soft running shoes stampede around her as she curls into a ball. A foot hits her ribs and launches off her. Feels kind of good. Reminds her of basic training. It's been ages since she's had a massage. Fun is having its way with her.

"Sorry."

"What the—"

"Hey!"

She is jerked to her feet and draped over a huge firefighter's shoulders. He's running with a tank of air on his back and a firefighter's mask strapped to his face as he drops her off on the other side of the street. Placed firmly on her feet, she looks into his mask, and makes out a scowl.

"You okay." Not really a question, more of a statement, and then he's gone.

Christine ignores the approaching volunteer on the other side.

Her official-ness comes from a neon pink cap and matching fanny pack. Christine checks her phone. It's 10:01. She breaks into a sprint, careering down the crowded sidewalk, down an alley, and into the next street. A car honks at her as she flits across. She can see Too's crowded patio.

She slows to a walk about one hundred metres away and stops in the shadow of the huge cathedral. Joey served there a long time ago. This was before he got as far away as possible from religion, a challenge for a Catholic priest.

She scans the street for his short, spry frame and black ball cap. There's no Joey. Her heart is racing from the sprint. Now it skips as the heat from her body mixes with the chill of fear rushing in. There is no one else she can talk to about this thing. There is no one she can talk to at all. About anything. She has no friends. Foster care and a military career didn't produce a social butterfly. Three of the only real friends she had died that day when she was such a big fucking hero.

Joey isn't afraid of her. Not even a little. And now he's not here. Because she blew it.

He couldn't have gotten far.

The trendy, socially conscious coffee shops are full. E-bikes are leaned up against concrete water features with long grasses. She turns and looks at the cathedral, up at its golden-tipped spires. Maybe he went inside to pray.

She turns back around toward Too. Now she sees Joey walking toward her with an iced Vietnamese coffee in each hand. He stops on the edge of the shadow. Still in the sun, his eyebrows rise up past his sunglasses. He breaks out into silent laughter at the sight of her.

She feels a grin growing on her own face. All will be well. Her heart is beating in her ears. Her pants are clinging to her sweaty thighs and have gone transparent against her skin. Her blouse is untucked, and her bra will most likely dry last. Her hand has left a bloody dirtprint on her pants. She hasn't brushed her teeth.

Joey stops laughing and is beside her in the shadow. He gestures for her to take a coffee. He puts both coffees down on the sidewalk and takes his sunglasses off, as if to get a better look.

"Joey. Joey. I messed up, Joey."

"Okay okay okay. It's okay. You're okay." She's soaking wet and shaking. More like shuddering.

"No it's not okay. I killed someone last night, Joey. With my bare hands, and buried him in my graveyard." Suddenly she's babbling.

Joey gently grasps Christine's shoulders. "I'm here. I'm here. Let's get you sitting down. Okay. Here we go. We're moving, we're on the move."

All park benches were removed long ago from the downtown core. Joey guides her toward a concrete water feature, but realizes its lip is far too skinny to sit on, even for the skinniest downtown junkie. He sits her down on a cement ledge beside Too's various dumpsters. A haze of flies is competing over something in the nearest bin.

There is some privacy from Too's patio because of the wooden lattice that screens their customers from the alley. The patio is bigger than the restaurant itself. People are already on the patio eating bowls of Too's noodle soup even though it's barely ten thirty in the morning.

Joey saunters back over to the coffees and scoops them up. Christine can tell he is pondering her situation. Joey throws his shoulders back and fixes her with a long look. She can see he has a plan.

She manages to get the straw into her mouth after poking herself in the face a few times. She takes a sip of the cold, creamy, rich coffee. Her throat is dry. She went full out to get here. It's been a while. She swallows a few times. Joey sits down beside her.

"It was almost instant."

Joey sips silently and nods.

"He came for confession. It was sometime after eight."

"Who?"

"Terry. He's in recovery for addiction. Well, not really. He's a dealer who flits around recovery programs. He's done time. His wife came looking for him with his baby after."

"I see."

Christine continues. "He was in the grip of something ... powerful. We were side by side on the couch."

"Okay."

"He was going to choke me—or I don't know, it was fast, and the next thing I know I'm on my feet and he's out cold. I mean, out for good."

"Wow," is all Joey says. He's making loud sucking sounds as he patiently hoovers up the last drops of coffee. He begins to strategically stab his straw along the bottom to get every last drop.

"Joey."

"Yeah."

"What am I going to do?"

"What do you mean? It sounds like you took care of the body."

Joey tosses his coffee cup in a dumpster. A public recycling faux pas has been committed, and Christine feels eyes on them now. She cranes her neck to see an eater's head quickly turn back to his gluten-free noodles. Christine gets up and fishes the compostable cup out of the dumpster. Her blouse under her armpit is now smeared with coagulated fish sauce. She can see what the flies are feasting on. It's a blob of meat that's oozed out of a bag.

She walks around to the entrance of the patio with the offending cup, weaving through the occupied tables on her way to the garbage-sorting station. She drops the cup into the correct receptacle while trying to assess if the patrons might have been able to hear her and Joey. She thinks it's okay.

Back in the alley, she faces Joey, taps her ear, and points toward the tables. Joey nods. Now, in a barely audible whisper, Joey mouths his words very slowly. He looks like a cartoon character with his big eyebrows. "What about the murder weapon?"

She almost laughs. "It's sorted," she says.

"What was it?" he says in a more normal tone of voice.

"One of my altar candlesticks."

"How many times did you hit him? Just once?"

"Yeah, just once."

Joey can't help it, he breaks out in a grin. "Must have been quite the blow."

"Yeah." Christine is nodding slowly. "That set is big. Bigger than most."

"Sure. I'm picturing something like a small baseball bat?"

Christine tilts her head to the side. Grinning now.

"Yeah, sure. Except for the dead guy instead of a home run." She stops grinning. "Should I go to the police?"

"What do you think?"

Christine reconstructs the scene and reviews. When Terry came at her, it wasn't good. The light was gone from his eyes. There was no Terry. There was something else. Hollywood tries to capture this. She has seen it in her rifle scope. "No."

"No then."

"No!"

"That's right. No way. There's your answer."

"Okay, okay, will you absolve me though?"

"Yeah. Then I've got to go."

Christine feels relief. A little relief. But still, there's Shawna. Shawna showing up wasn't great. Christine starts moving toward the cathedral.

"Where are you going?" Joey's voice booms. Amplified. Enormous. The noodle eaters all look over. A young man has noodles dangling from his mouth. He's paused in mid-dangle.

"To the church," Christine responds.

"Take off your shoes"—Joey now appears twelve feet tall—"Get on your knees."

Christine sees patio people putting their bowls down and moving to get a better view. They should. Joey is the real deal. Christine takes off her shoes and tosses them aside. She falls to her knees in front of Joey. Despite the crunching impact of kneecaps on concrete, she makes no sound.

"Ouch," cries out a particularly empathetic onlooker. His companion shushes him.

Joey administers the ancient rite of absolution. The smell of garbage and grease wafts through the warm air. A siren screams by. They're no match for Joey. Loving the audience, Joey stands very erect, his jaw set, his eyes bright, as he finishes with the Latin: "In nómine patris, et filii, et spíritus sancti."

He winks at her as he helps her up. "It's all sacred ground, Christine."

BACK AT HER CAR, Christine leans against the driver's side door as crowds of happy fun runners flow past her, dressed in their best tees and spandex. She watches men and women openly flirting, sharing their race stories.

"I cracked my record," one pretty boy exclaims to his glowing friend.

Teams of colleagues, students, and families flutter by. This is Mars for Christine, an entirely foreign land—she is a no-fun zone. Ever since her family was killed in a car accident, she became expert at tuning out family fun. All these folks full of the joy of running, that's not the problem. The problem is the absolution didn't take. She can feel that she is unforgiven.

Something is festering deep inside her, like the bag of meat in the dumpster. It's not the small fragment of gravel embedded in her skinned palm. It's the small black stone stuck in her heart.

She's surrounded by happy people. She can't possibly back the car out, never mind drive away. Bright colours, flushed cheeks, and smiles everywhere she looks. She turns around and faces a pub. A Scottish pub that means business. Polished brass and solid wood. A serious drinking establishment.

Her grimy thumb presses down on the gleaming brass door handle. There's a click. The heavy oak door opens, and she steps through. This is the gateway, the gateway to pure happiness.

The first thing she sees is a barkeep polishing a glass. He's tall, and his broad shoulders offer nice resting spots for her head, but so what? That's her glass he's touching. He needs to stop polishing that glass and put something in it for her. Right now.

"Springbank. Neat."

He pauses, looks squarely at her, nods. She can't read the look. His eyes are like windows to the outdoors. Just clouds and sunshine. Maybe some ocean. Fuck him and his eyes of the great outdoors. Enough of all that already. She needs a drink. And that's his job. He turns to get the bottle. It's taking him long enough. Christine looks up at the wall of alcohol. She doesn't really want Springbank—not really in the mood to sip. She wants a gallon of vodka, cold vodka. She wants to hear ice in the glass, and she wants to drain the potent colourless liquid fast.

She spots a nice bottle of New Zealand Sauvignon Blanc in the wine fridge but stops herself from pointing and saying, "Me that too." She orders a glass from the barkeep and reaches for her wallet. Which isn't there. Her heart lurches. Where is it?

The very handsome bartender brings her the drinks. The first drinks after a long walk in the desert.

"I seem to have forgotten my wallet."

The bartender leans over the bar, as if to whisper to her. She leans toward him.

"Normally, I'd put these on the house for you."

Christine looks down. Her bra is indeed drying last. She can smell the fish sauce.

"Please don't take this the wrong way, luv." The whisper lowers further. "You look like an escapee from the loony bin."

Christine notices the drinks are still within reach. Easily.

"I mean, don't get me wrong."

Christine turns her attention from the drinks to him. So hot. He's grinning. Mischievous and kind.

"You, um, definitely have a look going on for sure. All white. Semi-transparent. Er, very intriguing, I'm shocked I haven't asked you if you're single." The grin breaks into a radiant smile, "But you're scaring the locals, luv."

Christine looks down the bar at the chronics. He's right. Those who have managed to pull themselves onto a bar stool this early can't handle conflict, let alone be near it. They can't deal with loonies, or just people for that matter. They can't buy groceries. They can't keep relationships. They can't digest food. Most of them probably can't wipe their asses. They can't do much. All they can do now is drink.

"Let me walk you to your car." He's quickly on the other side of the bar, offering an arm. "Mel, you're in charge while I walk this fine lass to her car."

Watery-eyed Mel grunts his approval. "That'll cost you a pint."

"Aye."

Quickly and with dignity, Christine is led out to her car.

"Pardon me." He slips his hand into her pocket to get her keys. Now he is coming close. Closer. He comes close enough to smell her breath. He's checking whether she's been drinking already.

He tucks Christine into her Honda, fastens her seat belt, reaches between her legs to pull on the handle that sends her seat sliding back. He leans in farther. Apparently, he has something to say to her. She doesn't really mind. This is the most intimacy she's had in years. His index finger presses down on the inside of her forearm, hard. It almost hurts. She looks down.

Her sleeves are rolled up. Some of her tattoos are visible. His finger is drilling hard into her tiny AA tattoo. He waits for her to look down. She does. He removes his finger and places it onto a gold AA pendant around his neck. Tapping it. His mouth is stern.

"A meeting then. There's one in fifteen minutes, big old church. Ten blocks that way. I'll make room for you, luv. Off you go."

He's already shut the door on her muttered thanks. Despite the heat, she wants the windows closed. She starts the car and cranks the AC. Above the fans she can hear him stopping traffic in his Scottish brogue. "Make way for the lass," he booms.

A path slowly opens up before Christine as she follows his directions back to her own church.

WARRANT SETH KASSMAN'S last watch as a military police officer has been uneventful, just like all his many shifts on watch for all the years he's served. That's one way to describe his career, uneventful. He takes weekends so the guys can do the family thing. Walter is out on rounds, so he has the place to himself. This job is mostly symbolic because there is no such thing as military policing when the troops are at home in Canada. Actual policing only happens on deployments outside the country, and he's never been deployed. For twenty years, he's been doing a whole lot of nothing. But not for much longer—today is his last day.

Radios are charged. Pens replenished. Pencils sharpened. Small arms locker correct. Windows, keyboards, and microphones clean—he sterilized them with his handy little bottle of sterilizing spray. Seth has refilled the log with enough sheets for next week. No one ever does that. He does that. Someone better start doing it when he leaves.

The leftover cake from his goodbye party is still in the fridge. Toothless Tracy had brought it out with candles lit. Like it was his birthday. She makes him sick. They sang "For He's a Jolly Good Fellow." He cringes at the thought that she might have breathed on his cake.

She had cornered him during the festivities. Frozen burgers done on a gas barbeque. No time for charcoal on a public service lunch break. Pop. No Beer. Not allowed beer any more at work barbeques. Stale chips, floppy plates. Someone fetched a potato salad from the galley. No plastic forks, only knives. Blobs of potato and mayo slowly soaked through the thin plates during the mandatory speeches.

"We're all here for you, Seth, you meathead." Tracy put a hand on his thigh, and his toes curled in his boots. She couldn't manage to get her hand around his thigh to squeeze. She gave up and patted it instead. He knows what he's doing in the gym. His legs are huge.

She doesn't get to call him meathead. Only people in uniform get to use that term. If he did that, if he ever touched that … thing, laid a hand on Tracy, he'd be written up. If he called her a term of endearment, he'd be written up. Double standard. Makes him sick. Her nicotine stains. Overpowering body odour. Dirty fingernails. Nauseating.

That was the typical Canadian bureaucratic send-off. Next week. Next week the boys are giving him his proper wetdown at the strippers. His last hurrah. It will be glorious.

A stupid fly buzzes in through the security window, thuds around, looking for an exit. How is it they can get in but not out? All five feet two inches of Seth jumps up from his seat. He grabs the fly swatter. It is also clean. He cleans it. The guys won't do stuff like that. Many people don't. They prefer to just let the dirt of life build up around them.

The fly swatter won't be staying pristine. Not for long. Seth waits until the filthy thing comes lower. It's beyond his reach. Lower. Lower. He's going to smash it into the beyond.

When Seth pulls back the swatter to inspect his kill, the dispatch printer catches what's not stuck on the window, and the fly's oozing carcass leaves a streak on a recent message.

Seth looks down. The glob of fly has fallen further, into the workings of the printer. He's going to have to get that out. All of it. Take it apart and clean it.

He sees a name on the message. Christine Wright. For the first time since his diagnosis, he feels a little rush of anticipation, a hint of something good in his future. That dumb bitch Wright. Thinks she's hardcore. He smiles and rips the message from the printer.

Fly guts are on the window and on the swatter and are beginning to dry. If fly guts are left like that, it makes them difficult to get off. They can adhere like glue. Seth doesn't care. He just keeps rereading the message. This is too good to be true. That spoiled bitch, handed everything on a platter. She made him look like an idiot a few years back. Little Miss I-can-do-it-better-than-anyone. Let's see if he can return the favour. Dirty bitch.

Seems her place of employment is involved in a missing persons alert. Military Police cannot respond to any civilian calls unless there is a military member involved. And she is. That's why the message popped up on the printer.

Seth has never gone out on a call before. He's a glorified bloody security guard, trained for everything under the sun, only nothing ever happens.

Seth blazes past Walter, who has just come in the door, ramming him with a shoulder as he charges by the poor chump.

"Sorry, Walter, I'll explain later."

Seth climbs into a Military Police car, a Ford Interceptor. She won't be happy to see him pulling up. No, Little Miss Invincible is about to meet her match.

MRS. INGRID DEE hustles toward the office door to check on the candlestick. She had hoped the walk would clear her head, but with each step she is more and more outraged. It is windy, and the young magnolia tree seems to be trembling in sympathy with her.

She left the candlestick in ketchup, catsup, whatever the blasted stuff is called. A vile condiment, full of sugar and dye, but most useful for dilemmas just like one they are facing now, this crisis with their precious altarpiece candles. She left the vat in the office overnight for the foul stuff to eat away at the tarnish, but it is as if the surface of the silver has not simply been tarnished, it's been changed. If anyone can bring that beautiful piece back from the dead, it will be her.

People don't value heritage any more. They don't even know the meaning of the word. Their heads are full of distractions. They don't know what happened last week let alone twenty years ago. That altarpiece is very old and hails from Norwich—in England. Alight, it burns with the presence of peace. Her mother told her that it had been lit by Julian of Norwich, the female mystic who wrote about her visions back in the Middle Ages.

Amid plague, war, and intense suffering, Julian didn't wallow, Julian prayed. Julian chose to seek the light. And just what does this Reverend do with this beautiful symbol of human resilience? This beacon of hope in the face of mayhem? Well, that's the question, isn't it? What on earth did she do to it? Why was she trying to clean it when she, Mrs. Dee, the keeper of the candlesticks, had just polished them to perfection? It beggared understanding.

And let us not neglect the missing rug. It has, under Reverend Wright's care, simply vanished. Gone in the night.

Mrs. Dee's hands are shaking. This is a most dire situation. She fumbles for the keys, somewhere in the depths of her purse. Unnecessarily, it appears, since the back door opens with a mere nudge. Mrs. Dee stands where the rug used to be, pulling her sweater more tightly around herself. The Reverend probably left the door unlocked. That's how the rug vanished. That girl just will not take directions about anything. Pure arrogance.

Now here she is, hauling a long metal ladder, banging it into the back door jam, her sharp cheekbones flushed pink and her dark raven hair flying every which way.

"Happy Easter to you, Mrs. Dee!"

"Yes, Reverend, same to you. Now, just where on earth are you going with that?"

"Into the church—can you go ahead and open the door for me?"

That idiot girl, what on earth is she up to now? Can't she just leave them in peace? People don't want change. They want what they know. Mrs. Dee lets out a sigh and wrenches the door open with unnecessary force, banging her own hip so hard she gasps. In the small transept, Christine extends the ladder to its full height, leans it up against a rafter, and before Mrs. Dee can object, scrambles up to where the British flag hangs.

"Please do enlighten me, Reverend, just what is it that you are doing?"

"No flags in church, Mrs. Dee."

"But you can't!"

"Mrs. Dee, with respect, I'm not discussing it."

"Queen and Country!" Mrs. Dee cries in a squeaky voice she doesn't recognize as her own.

The Reverend comes clambering down the ladder, flag in hand. She begins to fold the flag, which is covered in years of dust. The Reverend is most careful in her movements, not allowing the flag to touch the ground, and she puts it carefully on a pew.

With smudges of dust on her black blouse, Christine moves the ladder as if the great clunky thing weighs nothing. The Canadian flag is obviously next.

"Please forgive me when I ask you, just what gives you the right?" Mrs. Dee can feel a red blush breaking out across her neck and chest.

"I'm qualified."

"Is that so?"

"Yes." Christine looks up and adjusts the ladder.

"May I ask just why that is?"

"The medal that I was awarded last week in Ottawa." She looks past Mrs. Dee, toward the front door. "That qualifies me."

Mrs. Dee, who adores the royal family, knows exactly who else was in Ottawa last week. And probably for the last time in her reign. This girl is trim as a soldier, and that's no surprise, but these wars lately are hardly what anybody in their right mind should be calling a war. Pushing people around in their own homes. Now her father, he knew real war. He knew the horrors of World War II.

"Do you mind if I ask what the medal was awarded for? Pardon me for not being apprised of this. For my own sanity I have been on a media fast since the vaccines were produced. The media tends to go on about their own agenda a great deal, don't you agree? Makes it so difficult for us to get any kind of proper information."

The Reverend makes eye contact. Her grey eyes glint, unflinching. Mrs. Dee catches her breath. She can almost see her with a rifle in her hands, using it.

"I don't talk about it." Christine is halfway up the ladder. "No flags in church," she says, and it's a command.

Mrs. Dee swallows hard, her mouth suddenly very dry.

THE CANDLESTICK *is in its correct place for Easter Sunday. Once part of a pair, its recent transition has now made it a singularity. Since its creation, things had never been this way.*

The women sensed this. One had polished and the other had made suggestions. There had been a prolonged bath in a sweet tomato sauce. They both worked as hard as they could, then lamented their thwarted efforts. No matter what either woman did, the dull blackening persisted. Still, the candlestick remained at the heart of the rite, as it should. The Lord has risen indeed.

The server will light from the presence lamp, which had been so carefully watched over by a woman, be it only for a few hours. The flame did go out not long after her departure. The woman fixed that with a lighter the next day. Lime green in colour. This could be considered a vulgarity. It is not. What matters is that it was relit. What matters is that it burns. Brightly. Darkness shall not overcome it.

This candlestick pair was one of thirty sets commissioned for the churches in Norwich in an effort to furnish the rebuilding of Christ's Church after the Norman invasion.

Armouries demanded the newer, longer swords for fighting. The father could not yet make them. This was not important. His gifts lay with the patience to craft great detail into metal.

The artistry cannot be exceeded. They were forged by the members of one family of craftspeople, all of them grateful to have lived through all the marauding pillage and knowing they would eat, thanks to the commission.

The boy knew his lessons and conceived the theme. The girl could draw. The mother sharpened a number of sticks for her daughter.

In the evenings, when the forge was cooling, they would gather in the dwindling dusk. The father and the boy smoothed out a palette in the sand. The daughter listened and drew. The mother insisted the chamomile of Isaiah didn't look like a weed. The father laughed when the detail got too wild. The boy brought it all together.

They ended their work in prayer. They prayed for God to work through them. And for safety from all the horrors of this world. Pride, blindness, vainglory, greed, hatred, and violence. AMEN.

TOM ISN'T FEELING this Easter thing. He shifts in his stiff dress shoes, which he bought for serving at this church. Can't serve the Lord in your sneakers.

Guess Jesus is resurrected today. But then he left again or something like that. Tom doesn't know. He's just going through the motions. Fake it till you make it. It's cool.

Christine knows. She knows he's not a Christian. Maybe he is. Grandma made sure he got the holy water on the forehead when he was a baby. He's just bringing the body, hoping his mind will follow.

He went through that messed up Maundy Thursday thing. The long, depressing Good Friday stuff. Stayed up late on Saturday night. Took time off from the autobody shop so he could do all this stuff during their Holy Week. And today is the day. The big deal is supposed to happen today, Easter Sunday. Tom hopes so. He wants a spiritual experience. He needs one. That's why he's here in this church, trying to get one of those.

The church is old and made of stone. Looks like a postcard of a museum. He's used to churches with lots of life inside. Singing, food, kids running around. No kids here. Just the old ladies. These old biddy church ladies. There's one old dude. He's cool. He gives the ladies a hard time. Likes to upset people. It's funny. The old ladies are all dressed up in bright colours and wearing hats. One hat definitely is not for keeping the sun off the face. It is stuck onto the side of her head, with birds and multicoloured eggs perched on the crown.

He wonders what his little girl is doing today, back in California with her status-obsessed mother. She's just four, and her last birthday card came back to him unopened. That hurt. He should send her a picture of him today. Here he is with the Anglicans. Wearing a smock, not one but two of them. A black one under a white one. He looks like a clown. Many buttons on the black one. Not in a million years did Tom think he would ever be wearing smocks and lighting candles. Christine makes it okay though. She's legit.

She doesn't nose around. She's not trying to get anything out of him. Or anyone. Different kind of bird. Kind of pretty, but she doesn't seem to know it. Never a hair out of place. Always watching but doesn't join in. At AA meetings she never partook in "fellowship." Then one day out come descriptions of her spiritual experiences.

Her spiritual experiences sounded too hard. He hopes God goes easier on him. He asked her out. She looked at him and said no. It's the best no he's ever got. When Christine looks at him, she sees all of him, who he really is.

It is time to light the candles on the altar. South then north. The north one is different today. It's dull and dark. It looks ugly. The details are almost gone. What's up with that? Is this an Easter thing? What is he supposed to do? Tom lights it and casually looks around. The church ladies are all at prayer already, eyes closed. Tom genuflects and returns to the office.

Christine is almost ready. She is murmuring prayers as she ties a narrow rope around her waist. He can tell that Christine is in a thin place. She goes there sometimes, but it's really obvious right before service.

The church ladies trained him to serve. They told him to call Christine Mother. This happened one time only.

"God gave you a mother, Tom, and it isn't me."

"Well, what should I call you?"

Slight grin. "High Priestess?" Watching.

"Is that a thing?"

"Christine is just fine, Tom."

Tom waits until she puts on the last layer. Deep purple cape with gold edging. Purple and gold. Regal. The gold cup is in use today. Everything looks good. Except for that one candlestick.

He checks over her robes. Nothing is out of place. It is 10:28 a.m., time to do their pre-service prayers. He cues her. "Prayers, Christine?"

She looks at him. Her grey eyes are like a light mist. "Yes, please."

He stands beside her at the long vestry dresser with a crucifix hanging above it. They confess their sins, love, and awe before a tortured Jesus on the cross. Carved in wood, the anguish on his face is intense.

Tom brings Christine his heavy-duty issues. Each layer of recovery is harder. Sometimes he feels like recovery is killing him. The healing is too much. With some breakthroughs, he feels grateful and frightened at the same time. It's confusing. Sometimes he can't take it.

Christine gets it. On those days, she listens. She goes quiet. Then she says the right words to him. Every time. The right words.

He asked once, "How are you doing this?"

She nodded in the direction of the wooden crucifix they are below now. "He's doing it."

"Okay. Yeah. But why then? Why are you helping me?"

"Because someone did it for me."

MRS. DEE ALLOWS her lower back to rest against the pew. Only during the sermon does she permit this. More and more she is drowning in thoughts. She used to have reprieves from this dreadful affliction of worry when she baked, cleaned, or gardened. That was before the pandemic. Before lockdowns. She thought that after things quieted down somewhat her nerves might do the same.

It is becoming more difficult to focus. Of course, the candlestick is most upsetting. She forces her eyes away from it. It is time to listen for the Word. She watches this tiresome female Reverend take her position at the pulpit.

This is a first for Mrs. Dee. A female priest. Another change. So many changes. The last rector changed all the plants on the grounds. His reason? Why, there was no money for expenditures such as those. Changed out all the roses for scrub. All of them. No more lawn. Cannot be seen to be wasting Earth's resources, so he shut off the irrigation system. Made sure the local newspaper saw him at pipeline protests.

Next was a most unpleasant game of musical chairs with the altar. For Eucharist they began to gather in a circle. Most undignified. His wife, who oversaw the slaughter of the roses, also decided she was to bake the bread. A crumbly mess that loaf was, her attempt at gluten-free.

One Trinity Sunday, at the most dramatic part of the Eucharist, the moment when the body of Christ is broken, the priest raised it and it crumbled—everywhere. The bell-ringer looked bemused as the words of consecration ceased. Determined, the priest collected all the crumbles for them.

That day the bread of heaven was more like the bread of the parking lot. Mrs. Dee thanked God when the clean, crisp, perfectly circular, thin wafer was placed in her empty hand the following Sunday. Albeit while still standing in a circle.

The entire place was beginning a descent into chaos. The organ is kaput. Terribly expensive to repair pipe organs. The game fence has a hole in it that's held together with twine. Twine is a joke to most deer. Gone is their outdoor lighting. She had warned Mr. Crumbles. She had warned everyone. The wild of the park—unless it's kept back, the wilderness will encroach and eventually take over. Just as she thinks this, a chipmunk scurries along the wall beneath the stained-glass window of the fishes and loaves.

This mental babble never takes her anywhere anyway. She must focus. Just stop all this ruminating and listen for the Word, Ingrid. The Word. This Word that was with God and then came into the world—that Word. The Word that darkness won't overcome. She prays to hear what she is supposed to hear. Loudly. Above all the chatter of her mind.

Mrs. Dee has done this for most of the Sundays of her life. She has heard it all. She has been called both a sacred vessel of life and a whore from that pulpit. Not her personally, but her gender.

Once when the hypocrisy was just too thick to breathe, she staged a dramatic exit, mid-sermon. Everyone knew that the venerable what'shisname was having sexual intercourse with a seventeen-year-old. Everyone knew, including his wife, who always sat in the first pew. What Mrs. Dee couldn't stomach was that he had carried on for over twenty minutes about monogamy, which he knew nothing about.

Her husband knew the priest was being untoward. Norman was a good man. She leaned over to whisper that she was leaving. He whispered back that he would see them at home. Mrs. Dee pulled her daughter out of the pew. She spun them both around and processed out of that church, her heels hammering the floor on her way out. Now that's an exit.

After his dementia came on, Norman's carefree attitude disintegrated into shouting and petulance. Mrs. Dee would visit him after services today, in the care home. Finally, she is allowed to touch him on their visits. After months of no visits, he does not know her, which is difficult.

Mrs. Dee forces herself into the present. She watches the Reverend's mouth—she's saying something about Mary Magdalene. Mrs. Dee is hardly surprised by this. Magdalene is all the rage right now. First she's Christ's wife, next she's the whore of the world, now she's an occult figure. The Reverend lands the point she's been heading toward. The girl does honour the Word. She'll give her that. It is speaking right to her. Through her. In her. The dignity Mary Magdalene sought to bring her beloved in death. This is the point. This is what brings Mary to the tomb. And it cannot happen.

The Reverend possesses good elocution. "Where is he, Mary asks the gardener. Where has he been taken?"

Mrs. Dee's eyes fill with tears. She cannot swallow the grief she knows so well. At first, they tried to reach him. Then they gave up. Now they keep him chemically unreachable. She was told that it is safer for everyone and that he is easier to care for. Half the time, he's not in his room. They just wheel them into a holding area, with any luck pointed toward a window. The kindest of the young and healthy care aides look over from their phones occasionally.

She doesn't know where her beloved is. She doesn't know where they've taken him.

CHRISTINE IS SHAKING hands at the door—they are taking their time making their way out—and her smile feels like a rictus. Eleven people including herself on Easter Day. This must be some sort of record. Shawna and the baby arrived during the psalm. That makes thirteen.

The child had squawked and chirped throughout the service. Christine didn't mind. Mr. Fowler did. Normally, he expends his vindictiveness all over her while saying goodbye. Like a fire hose. She shakes his hand and braces for impact.

"I couldn't hear anything because of the screaming brat." He speaks loud enough for Shawna to hear and jerks his hand away from Christine's like he's repelled by her touch.

Shawna is next, surrounded by a thick cloud of dirty-diaper smell. Christine can almost taste it. Judging from the look on the faces of the two women behind Shawna, so can everyone else. Shawna is pale, thin, and her long hair is greasy.

"Didn't hear from you yesterday." She shifts the fussing child to the hip nearest Christine.

"Right. Did you call?"

"Uh, yeah, I did. Also, I should tell you something."

"Why don't you come for the parish Easter supper tonight?"

"No. I want to be at home. In case, you know …"

"What about tomorrow?"

Shawna eyeballs her. "A lot of people said Terry was at your place. Why are they saying that?"

"Well, that's interesting. Let me say goodbye and we'll look into it, okay?" Bloody hell.

"Fine. I'll be outside."

Shawna leaves a brown fug behind her, and Christine watches the last people to pass try to evade it, pressed up against the door frame opposite Christine. The very last is Mrs. Wilson, a slow-moving, short, and stout woman who looks like an owl with her round glasses and her all-knowing expression. When you talk to Mrs. Wilson, it's like a game of charades, where a raised eyebrow might be the only clue she gives to her meaning. Today, she looks as if to say something life-changing, inspiring. So, with a whisper into Christine's ear, out it comes.

"A fine Easter service." Christine smiles as if this is a wonderful surprise.

"Happy Easter, Mrs. Wilson."

Mr. Fowler has lain in wait for Shawna in the parking lot. Christine joins them.

"I come to pray, not to hear a screaming brat or smell its filth."

"Yeah. Super holy. Get away from me."

"No. You get away from me. From here. From us. Don't come back until you've learned how to change a diaper. How to be a mother. Disgraceful."

"Mr. Fowler, I'm asking you now to get into your car and leave."

"I will not, Reverend. I've probably paid for this parking lot. A few times over. I'll leave when the spirit moves me."

"I've just put a pot of tea on in your office." Mrs. Dee appears from the direction of the church. "I'll fetch some of my cookies. Your desk makes a fine change table."

Shawna mumbles her agreement, and Shawna and Christine turn toward the path beside the church. Mrs. Dee walks Mr. Fowler to his car. The sun is shining, and light is bouncing off the pools of rainwater.

Mrs. Dee catches up with them. The flower beds along the edge of the church are showing the first colours of spring. Christine looks over to the right and notices a crow drinking from a pool of water on Terry's grave, just a couple of metres away. Mrs. Dee's voice makes Christine flinch.

"Do be careful, Reverend!"

"Mrs. Dee?"

"The beadwork, Reverend."

Christine realizes she's been clutching her bible to the beadwork on her chasuble.

"Of course."

"I'll bring you and Shawna some cookies. You have your keys?"

"Yes, thank you, Mrs. Dee."

Mrs. Dee keeps walking to the residence as Christine unlocks the back door of the church. Once inside the office, Christine carefully removes the fine chasuble, then quickly removes all the other layers of ceremonial clothing, leaving her in a short-sleeved collared shirt and slacks.

Christine pours two mugs of tea. They're not really mugs, more like really big teacups. Mrs. Dee doesn't allow mugs. She doesn't like them. Fine. Whatever.

"Milk? Sugar?"

"Two and two."

Christine hands Shawna her big cup of tea. Because of its size, the handle is strange. It's too thin for the size of cup attached. The baby is lying belly down on the floor, kicking her heels and waving her arms like a little swimmer. The baby is on the wood floor because there is no more rug. Mom and babe are right where Terry was lying a few nights ago.

Shawna takes two quick slurps, puts her cup on Christine's desk, and picks the child back up for no reason. The child begins to cry. There is a spot of Terry's blood right beside Shawna's cup on the desk. Shawna is bouncing the baby, trying to stop the incipient crying.

"I never wanted her."

Christine does her best not to stare at the blood.

"I thought it would be good. You know. Fix things. With Terry."

As if on cue, the baby lands one on Shawna's face. Half grab, half punch. Good one, Baby. Shawna is trying to get some strands of her ridiculously long hair out of the baby's fist.

"Their nails are sharp. Did you know that? So this guy said Terry came here on Friday."

Tom bursts through the door from the church. Still in his cassock and surplice.

"Am I interrupting?"

"No, Tom. Go ahead and finish up. Tom, this is Shawna. I think you might already know each other."

"We haven't met in person." Shawna's voice is suddenly silk. Baby and Shawna are now cooing. Magic. Even though he's wearing a dress, pretty much, some things are very clear about Tom. He's tall, good looking in a street-scarred way, and kind. Tom is a catch.

He puts the large altar candlesticks on the desk. He turns around.

"May I?" Tom takes the baby from Shawna. The baby smiles up at him.

"What's your name?" he coos.

"Terrine," Shawna says coyly. "She just loves men!"

Shawna picks her tea back up off the desk. Terrine has little to say. Especially about being named after a French meat delicacy.

"Terry named her." Shawna is trying to sweep her hair behind her ears, as if that would suddenly make her hair look clean.

Christine sits back in her office chair. She looks away from Shawna at the couch under the window. Terry must have come up off his feet. Christine feels the strain in her right arm. The ache runs all the way through. Close to the bone.

She looks at her right hand as it grips the too-thin handle on her large teacup. Her pinky is doing the balancing. She stretches her index finger alongside the handle as if on the trigger guard of a rifle.

There's a knock at the back door. Everyone falls silent and looks over. Even Terrine. Could be Mrs. Dee with hands full, knocking with her foot. Kicking the door with her foot is not really like her though.

Getting up from her chair, Christine decides it can't be Mrs. Dee. This is a power knock. A knock that says open right now, or else.

Christine opens the door and blinks at the sight of two law enforcement officers, one short and one her height with a grim look on his face. Military Police and Royal Canadian Mounted Police. The MP looks agitated and like he gets a haircut every morning. The Mountie looks calm and like he gets a haircut once a week. They both start talking. The Mountie stops and lets the MP carry on.

The MP is so short that she fights the urge to go into a partial squat to look him in the eye. She knows him. He's a dick. That little asshole threw her in the cells when she was a brand new recruit. Little tough guy. Tried to scare her. Why is he even here? They don't let MPs do civilian policing. She's a civilian now.

MRS. DEE STANDS in the kitchen, about to open the cupboard where the cookies are kept. She has a key, as she should. The residence is part of the parish. Her parish! While the Reverend is busy with Shawna, why not take a few moments to poke around for the rug?

Mrs. Dee glances into the living room, looking for any inappropriate changes. Then she makes her way slowly back to the kitchen, thinking of Mr. Fowler. He is so hateful. The bitterness that courses through his veins must somehow preserve him—he is getting on in years and yet he looks like he always has, like a smooth-faced accountant. She pities anyone in his path.

Getting into his car, Mr. Fowler was almost spitting when he declared Shawna an unfit mother and probably a crackhead and other words she doesn't like to even think about. Mrs. Dee notices the recycling bin contains the missing paint stripper and rust remover from the shed. Both are completely empty.

Mrs. Dee picks up the containers. This girl needs to learn how to properly recycle. These jugs have had noxious substances in them. What on earth would the Reverend need with all of that? Now she'll have to order more, right away.

Deficiency and shortage bother Mrs. Dee. But this pales in comparison with the rug going missing. Mrs. Dee wonders if this is the same as the flags. Is the rug symbolic of something now out of fashion or no longer correct? It seems everything she holds dear is out of fashion. But not that rug. Things like that do not go out of fashion and are irreplaceable.

It was a lush garden. Anyone who walked on it felt the opulence. Most mistook it for Persian. It wasn't. It was hooked by the Women's Guild during World War II. Women sick with worry. Mothers, sisters, and wives who didn't know what to do with their hands. With themselves. They knew what was going on over there. No sense in talking about it. So they hooked that rug. Together.

Once the rug was finished, the war carried on. So they carved a relief into a small oak table. Then messages began to arrive. Most of their men were not going to return. Eventually, the rug was moved into the office. Her mother had been one of the women who hooked that rug. Her father had come home, for a while. Long enough to make her two younger brothers and her sister.

The darkness he had fought on the beach, in camps, and up through Caen. They all hoped that it had been extinguished over there. Across oceans. It wasn't. Darkness found him. It found all of them. And for what? What was that massive sacrifice for? Europe was quick to forget when they threatened sanctions on *their* vaccine.

In Christine's bedroom now, Mrs. Dee rips open the closet door, determined to find that blessed rug. That girl has simply forfeited any claim to privacy. The rug is not hers. She cannot do with it what she will. Why doesn't she just keep that office door locked? It's the one thing Mrs. Dee has asked of her.

She spots the royal arms on a small red box on the top shelf and opens it. She remembers doing the same in her father's closet all those years ago. This medal is different from her father's—it's heavier. He had a few campaign stars and an Order of the British Empire. She remembers the motto "For God and Empire." This one is a cross. She knows what it is. It is a Victoria Cross. Here she is, just like when she was a girl playing detective, sifting and sorting chaos, trying to make sense of it.

This is what the Queen gave Christine. She carefully puts the box with the medal in it back where it was. Mrs. Dee then makes her way to the attic, opens the hatch on the crawl space, and peers in. Nothing.

She's not a stupid girl. She seems quite upright. It's confusing. Why would she bother herself with something like the rug? Is the issue with original sin? Mrs. Dee returns to the kitchen and places a few of her cookies on a plate for Shawna and the Reverend.

Walking toward the office now with the cookies, she walks past two police cars parked outside the residence. Hope grips her. Maybe they've found it! Joy! What is anyone going to do with a church rug? She breaks into a trot.

"Have you found it? Please tell me you've found it!" Mrs. Dee shouts as she flings open the door.

"Ma'am. Please." A man in a black uniform with a red beret stands up from a chair. "We are conducting an interview here."

Mrs. Dee notices two things immediately about this police officer. He is squat as a toad. And he has an erection.

"Oh, I see. Well, I'm so pleased to see appropriate action is being taken. That rug is irreplaceable. Whoever would break in here and steal it ..." Mrs. Dee puts the cookies down on the vestment dresser. "I'm afraid I haven't brought enough cookies. I'll fetch some more."

The Mountie stands up. Acne-scarred. Average height. No erection. He gives Mrs. Dee a pleasant smile and then addresses the Reverend.

"I think we'll be on our way. We've taken up enough of your time. Here's my card. Please call with any information. Thank you for your co-operation."

"I'll go with you. I'll come make my statement now." The young woman, Shawna, gathers up her baby items. Tom hands her the child, and she makes for the door at speed.

Mrs. Dee discreetly watches the police through the window while Tom and Christine finish up cleaning the chalice and placing the linens in their soaking bath. Shawna drives off while the two officers stand squared off, as if arguing. The erectionless one seems to win because the shorty has his fists clenched and stands there while the other one hops in his cruiser and drives off.

"What do you say, Mrs. Dee?" Tom is putting away the chalice. He has already taken off his cassock and is in his jeans. He really shouldn't be touching the chalice while in that attire.

"I'm just relieved to see them finally taking some action. But what does that young woman have to do with it?"

"She's why the police came, Mrs. Dee. Her partner has gone missing."

That doesn't make any sense at all. "Why did they come here?"

"Because this is where he said he was headed the night he went missing."

"When was this?"

"Friday."

Mrs. Dee stops looking out the window and turns to face Tom. "Is that so?"

"Thank you for the cookies, Mrs. Dee. I'm going to get started on the ham for the parish supper." Christine edges past her in the direction of the door. "I'll see you over there, Mrs. Dee. Does the ham get cooked in the hall kitchen?"

"Yes, it does."

Tom says goodbye too, leaving Mrs. Dee alone in the office, pondering all that has happened. She shakes her head and tucks the golden key for the tabernacle into its place in the storage cupboard by the closet. The beautifully enamelled gold plate used for serving the Eucharist bread on Easter is stored beside the key. She refolds everything and takes a moment to inspect the chasuble, which seems to be fine, thank goodness.

How strange. Maybe the missing man took the rug. She pauses. That thought seems to be arranged the wrong way around in her head. Mrs. Dee allows herself one of her cookies and a brief sit-down.

It's already after one p.m. Time to get the fold-up tables set up in the parish hall. Get the side dishes warmed. Get the ham in. More people show up for the parish supper than the service. She'll pop over and see Norman before she begins.

Mrs. Dee ties a knot in the trash bag. It smells to high heaven. She regrets using up a whole, pricey compostable waste bag. The offending diaper is in no way compostable.

After locking up, she makes her way to the dumpster. She's surprised to see that the squat cop is still there, sitting in his car. He's watching her. Something is the matter with him. His face is oddly contorted. Does he hate her? Why ever would that be?

She smiles sweetly at him as the bag hits the bottom of the empty dumpster with a hollow thud. No rug there, obviously. He is still glaring at her. He is looking at her over the steering wheel. He looks hungry, like a wolf. She doesn't have time for these melodramas.

Maybe she should invite him? She takes a step toward the car, then his erection appears in her mind. She has taken one step and stops, frozen.

Maybe she is mistaken about this odd little fellow. His uniform is, after all, quite ill-fitting. Far too tight, pants will pucker. Or maybe he had one of those prolonged reactions to the little blue pill. Mrs. Wilson has told her all about these pills. She herself had no idea.

Mrs. Dee has now invested a great deal of her time on Easter Day thinking about the state of a man's penis. She turns back toward the church. She shifts on her feet. It's the same when she listens to St. Paul blather on about circumcision, relentlessly.

Paul's discourse on circumcision has always bothered her. More than that business in Timothy about women not having authority. According to this Reverend, Paul didn't write Timothy. This makes perfect sense to her—it's obvious. Timothy lacks that verbose brilliance. But Paul did write about circumcision. Even a genius like Paul got hung up on the male member.

The priest who married her and Norman had a lovely bass voice. Now she remembers how it was never the same listening to him after he blathered on about circumcision. Hearing that word, circumcision, that many times, in that fine speaking voice.

No. We are more than our genitalia. The matter of his poorly timed erection is neither here nor there. This young man shall be invited to the parish supper. She pivots to face the police car, and as if in response to her glance, the vehicle roars to life.

He revs the engine. Mrs. Dee stands transfixed as he tears out of the parking lot. Some gravel pings off the metal dumpster as he makes his dramatic exit. Mrs. Dee has, in her experience, seen much better.

THE NEXT DAY, Christine packs up some leftovers for Shawna. Someone brought blueberry muffins that remained unopened, so she throws those into the bag along with bits of the supper from last night. Their friends from the convent, the Sisters of Equanimity, outdid themselves.

She has everything except baby food. When Christine stands at the convenience store till, paying for the little jars of goop, the cashier has a look on his face, something close to a smirk. Is it her collar? Or maybe it's the baby thing, or she just has the word killer imprinted on her forehead. She knows that on a certain level, nothing is hidden.

That's why she's paying a visit to Shawna. For appearances. To look like she cares. She doesn't want to go to prison. Her life feels enough like a prison already, since she has no friends and, it seems, a growing list of enemies. She pulls up outside Shawna's place but doesn't get out of the car. She'd rather sit here and stare at the gravel that has replaced the lawn in front of the townhouse Shawna until recently shared with Terry.

Lawns are out of favour now. The last rector of her church replaced their lawn with some ecologically correct mix of plants. Some of these were poisonous, so Mrs. Dee had to uproot them and plant others. Can't have lawsuits from parents or pet owners. Mrs. Dee and Mrs. Wilson know everything about plants. Especially the poisonous ones. Every conversation between them seems to involve gardening or flower arrangements, and every one eventually ends up on the topic of toxic flora.

Christine hauls herself and the baby food and the church sup-per leftovers out of the car and toward the front door, where, as she gets closer, she sees a child's green beach pail, full of water and cigarette butts. So welcoming.

Christine sees Shawna through the screen door, and Shawna spots Christine. Shawna gets up, holds the door, and lets it slam behind Christine as she comes in. Then Shawna sits down at the table and busies herself rolling cigarettes. Christine spots the word organic on the tub of tobacco. Shawna puts her finger to her mouth to indicate that Terrine is asleep.

"Scalloped potatoes, ham." She lifts things out of the bag, hastily arranging each item on the table.

"I don't … uh … well, thanks."

Blueberry muffins. Pecan sweet potato casserole. Baby food.

"Why are you here, Reverend?"

"To bring you this. Just checking in." It seems she's taken the lid off the ham. She snaps it back on again, then cringes. Mustn't wake Terrine.

"Checking in," Shawna says flatly.

Christine pulls out a chair at the table. The chair legs dragging over brown squares interspersed with yellow diamonds. She sits beside Terrine's high chair, which is smeared with old food.

"How are you? Did you make a statement yesterday?"

Shawna is quiet. Her robe is a greyish dusty rose, maybe not the original colour. Shawna looks like she could use a shower.

"Which is it?"

"What?"

"Which is it, do you care about how I am, or if I made a state-ment?"

"Sorry. How are you?"

"I'm fucking terrible." Shawna's green eyes flash up from her coffee cup. She has not offered Christine any, though there's a full pot on the counter behind her.

"Is there anything you need? I mean anything else." She looks at the containers of food, which even to her look unappetizing.

"Childcare. I'm going back to work. Nursing. To keep me in all of this luxury."

"Did you try the Montessori?" She regrets this as soon as it's out of her mouth. Christine is still unfamiliar with some aspects of civilian life. What is paid for and what isn't. In some levels of the military, everything is provided for. When you join Special Forces, distractions just magically disappear. You become a member of a world where the mission becomes the most important thing in life. She misses that suddenly. She could use a bit of government-sanctioned mayhem at the moment.

"Uh, no. It's okay. I've got it covered. A girlfriend is opening a daycare in her basement."

"Convenient," Christine says in her bright, false voice.

Shawna stands up. Picks up the ham. Opens the lid. Grimaces. Closes it. Puts it down on the table and pauses. "Yes. Very convenient, Reverend. Sort of like this visit." She faces her. "Why don't you ask me what you really want to know? What did I say to the police? That's why you're here, isn't it?" She nods to the rest of the food. "That's why you brought all this garbage over here."

"It's not garbage."

"Well, it is actually, Reverend. Did you know that I'm vegan? No. It appears not."

Shawna picks up the baby food.

"And thank you for the gas station baby food. Terrine eats only organic." Her overly long and heavily manicured fingernails poke one edge of the blueberry muffins. Christine is hopeful.

"And this hydrogenated, mass-produced factory food just doesn't really help, Reverend. It doesn't help the fact that I have to go back to work now."

"Yes, it's not helpful. I'm sorry."

"Yeah, I just fucking said that, thanks."

"Maybe I shouldn't have come."

"No, you shouldn't of. But you're here now, so let's talk."

"Okay, that's a good idea."

"I don't need your affirmation or whatever."

"Right."

"So I sent Terry to a meeting, and this meeting is at your church."

"Church hall," Christine corrects her.

"Church hall. So where the fuck is he?"

"I don't know, Shawna."

"Yeah, I think you do know."

"You do."

"Yeah, I do. I talked to some people at the meeting. That military policeman told me to ask them, so I did."

"That's good. What did they say?" Christine couldn't care less what they said. Why is the MP even talking to Shawna? Telling her to snoop around? This is under the RCMP's jurisdiction. Great. This is just what she needs.

"They said that he left the meeting early and that he went to go find you."

"Hmm."

Shawna tightens her bathrobe around herself and asks, "Are you fucking him?"

Christine suppresses a laugh. She hasn't had sex in nearly eight years. Her last relationship was about as dysfunctional as two human beings can have. Best if this vagina stays closed for business.

"No, no, Shawna, that would be totally inappropriate, on so many levels."

"Was he there, when I was there?"

"When?"

"When do you think? Friday night. When me and Terrine came, was he there?"

"No."

"That's why you didn't invite me in, isn't it?"

"No, Shawna."

"Because he was there. Wasn't he?"

"Shawna, don't worry. They'll find him."

Shawna picks up a muffin and chucks it at Christine's face. Christine turns a little late and the muffin slams into her chin. Very durable muffins.

Shawna stands up and yells, "I know you're lying!" Christine sees another muffin in Shawna's hand. "Liar!"

Christine holds her hand up, like a bloody crosswalk guard. Ridiculous. She could take her down so easily. "Shawna, calm down."

"I'll calm down when you tell me what the fuck the two of you are up to."

"We're not up to anything." Not even heavy breathing. Or any kind of breathing, really.

"You're helping him. I know it!"

"With what?"

"Hiding him. From me. From the mob."

Christine turns around and feels the next four muffins bounce off her shoulders. She is out the door and lurching down the stairs when she catches her foot on the green ashtray pail and the cigarette butts gush out. She's about to stoop and try to clean up the sludge—with what though?—when another muffin hits her in the glutes. Finally, the last one in Shawna's magazine of baked goods hits the screen door.

"He can't hide forever!"

Not at only two feet under, Christine agrees. The aromas of the encounter fill the car. Old cigarettes meet fake vanilla with almost blueberry. She pulls away and wipes a crumb off her cheek. Fucking Terry. Wow. That's a no go. Especially now. Terry's not up for it. Not really up for much.

She's knocked the rear-view mirror askew scrambling into the car, and she glimpses her face. She begins to laugh, then stops. Not funny, Christine. She snorts. Okay, a bit funny. Shawna's street is lined with cherry trees. Christine's windshield has been lightly adorned with petals and they flit off as she drives toward the ocean. Dog walkers and kiteboarders move about the bluffs.

She must make the RCMP ignore Shawna. The MP was only there because she's Military. But she was done in January. She's a civilian. With slick efficiency, a filing drawer opens in her mind. These files contain every kind of leverage. Surviving requires good file maintenance. One must continually sift and sort the accumulated leverage on every human being encountered.

She tries to close it. Too late. Something ugly has slipped out. What if the cops knew about Shawna's addictions? What if the baby—no, don't go there. She's supposed to be helping people find peace. Find redemption. Find healing. She's supposed to be comforting those who suffer. The exploited. The hated. The ignored. She's not supposed to be driving around with ugly ideas slithering about her brain. Christine thinks about her savings. Not a lot there, but Shawna might like—no, no. Where would Joey be right now? Must find Joey.

THE CANDLESTICK *finds itself in a conundrum it has never before encountered. Some aspects are familiar. For one, it is on display, and its more polished partner is nearby. These parts of the puzzle are correct. However, there is no flame, and the location is utterly wrong. The setting is that of commerce. This is incorrect.*

There is a Sister of God nearby. But she is not adoring her Creator. She is instead attempting to revitalize her people. This Sister is collecting money at a rummage sale to support their work. The hard work of building relationship. With God, self, and other.

Adam, the clay person, the earth person, was not to be alone. Yes, God breathed life into Adam, but that was not all. Adam was to relate, to connect. The Almighty decided we were not to live alone. So came Eve. So came relations. So came breathing life into one another. Clay people, earth people, working themselves into life, life working into them. So it shall be forever.

Their light has lit a path for those who sought peace. To help those seek God as God seeks them. To reveal the pattern of sublime redemption already at hand.

The candlestick, despite its displeasure at being considered rummage, appears to be involved in this effort. Together, the set will fetch fifty dollars toward this aim. The sticker placed on both in the pair validates this assertion.

The novice had trouble making the price adhere to the base. There is good reason for this. The workmanship is beyond intricate. The feet appear like tree roots. Like a wild, unbegotten place of raw beauty.

Midway, the wilderness is transformed to a smooth pillar. Stunning and metaphoric.

A greedy bargain hunter disagrees.

"This one is almost ruined. Not sure if it will come back. If so, it's going to take a miracle."

He walks off with them after talking the Sister down to half price. This is a most sinister liturgy. AMEN.

SETH KASSMAN is clearing out his locker on the Easter holiday Monday. In the excitement of the call on Sunday, he forgot to do this, the last step of leaving his job. Sweet-ass retirement, here he comes. Full speed ahead.

He shouldn't waste that protein powder. He'll bring it home. It causes deadly farts but also huge gains in the gym—massive gains. Not that he can go to the gym any more. Man, he's got some choice magazines in his locker. Over the years, he's built up quite the collection. Sometimes he would bring dad's *Playboys*, with bush and real tits for the boys. He has porn from all over the world. The best was the Japanese animation with octopus tentacles penetrating every orifice in schoolgirls. Dirty, filthy girls. Then there was the expensive German stuff. Can't leave that behind. No way.

Of course he'll be leaving the mags behind along with everything else in this life soon. Maybe he should give them to Walter. He'd like that. Walter doesn't get the Japanese stuff though. He'd probably prefer the *Playboys*. Cartoons don't do it for the guy.

Seth thinks about Wright. She hasn't changed. Little Miss Wright. Smug, arrogant bitch. She's quite lean. The whole priest's collar thing doesn't do anything for her. It makes her creepier. Wright is a creep show.

He remembers Wright when she was brand new. She had just shown up from basic training when he threw her in the drunk tank. Feisty. Scrappy. The local Carson Club bouncer had called. "You need to pick up one of yours. You might want to bring a partner. She's, uh, a bit challenging."

It was after midnight. Midnight is a special time on the dance floor at the Carson Club. It's quite the sight. The DJ pulls all the girls looking for a meal ticket off their bar stools. These sluts are flexible. They work it. Their inner stripper comes out. They've got moves. They shake it. Tempting, slutty teases. A mating dance you see only in bars close by to military bases.

Seth has frequented some rough locales in his day. The Carson Club holds its own. The clientele, the music, the smell, the rough-and-tough staff. Raw and wild. Good fun, shit. But he would never touch any of those whores. Fun to watch. Like being at the zoo. The Carson Club is like the whore zoo.

So he picks up Wright and takes her to the cells. That's the small jail for idiots who break the rules. Not the rules in the civilian world, but military rules. He doesn't bring a partner. He doesn't need a partner to pick up a drunk little girl. She's docile at the bouncer's side and then quiet in the car. She won't make eye contact. She answers all his questions, uses rank, seems polite.

He gives her a good shove into her cell. She needs to be reminded that he's not a babysitter or a taxi driver. "Enjoy the rest of your night." He locks the cell and turns around to leave. He stops dead in his tracks at the distinctive sound of a magazine sliding out of a Sig Sauer service pistol. He searched her. He looks down—his holster is empty. What the fuck? No way. She didn't.

He turns around and looks at her through the bars. He grips the bars in panic. How the fuck did she do that? This is no fucking good at all.

She is sitting on her cot, humming and smiling. She slides the top assembly back to remove the chambered round. Like he's trained to do, like they are all trained to do. If someone finds out, it could be a career ender.

She knows that. She wants him to know that she knows that.

Stupid fucking cunt. Seth grips the bars tighter. His heart is racing. Who does she think she's playing with?

She hops off the cot at the back of the cell and moves toward him in a low crouch. It's like she's showing submission, except she's too quick and quiet as she spiders along the floor. Seth shivers. Fucking creep show.

She places his magazine and pistol with great care on the bare cement floor, easily within his reach. Taunting him. Humiliating him. Calling him a pussy. That's what she's doing.

He should make her pay. Make her sorry. He assembles his weapon and reholsters it.

He gets his keys out and puts the key in the lock. She's waiting for him, on her feet now. She makes eye contact. She looks like a severely injured animal. She wants him to come at her. She's ready and waiting.

Well, the creep show can keep waiting. He'll sort her out another time. Besides, she's so drunk she won't remember. He wants her to remember. He takes the key out of the lock.

That never made it to the summary trial, about his weapon. She was only charged for conduct unbecoming and public drunkenness. The normal things. If it had come out about his weapon, his charges would have been more severe than hers. You don't ever let a perp take your weapon. You don't ever let anyone take your weapon, let alone dismantle it. She crossed a line. That's fine. He'll get her back. He'll pick his moment.

A few years later he deduced that she went Special Forces. Her file came through for wiping. His office wipes any identifiers to facilitate clandestine operations. This is so that the "special" idiots, who think they are superhuman, cease to be accountable.

It's rare for the reverse to be done, for the identifiers to be reassigned to the record. This is because the term Special Forces really means Suicidal Freaks. Not a lot of those freaks retire. But Wright did. About five years ago, her service record came back into his office for a release procedure after she became a hero.

Princess Wright got a Victoria Cross, the first one since World War II. She got three of her guys killed saving some important asshole in the desert. She was being given a distinctive reintegration retirement. The royal treatment. Subsidized university, reintegration assistance, and vocational placement. They were going to try to make a human being out of her after all.

He read further into her file. He was curious what this freak show was going to be next. What did the civilian world have to look forward to? He chuckled when he read *ordained minister*. Unbelievable. He's not a religious man but that was not holiness he saw in that cell that night. He went to the base commander.

"Sir, with Wright, just finishing up her file. What about this conduct unbecoming charge?"

The base commander didn't care for that. He must be in her fan club.

"What charge?"

"Well, it's old."

"Warrant Kassman, that charge was to be expunged. All charges of that nature are expunged after two years. I'm baffled why you still have a record of it. Besides, do you really trust anyone who hasn't had a few charges?"

"I just wanted to be prudent, Sir. Considering her new vocation."

"What would be prudent of you is to get that record ready to go, Warrant. We set our people up for success. Especially people like her. Have it to me before you leave today."

"Yes, Sir."

That commander moved to another unit around the time of Seth's first diagnosis. Back when the doctors thought they could fight this thing. Come to think of it, he's getting a special retirement too. The pension people will dump his entire annuity, after taxes, into his bank account. That would have happened today, but it's Easter Monday.

Tomorrow, he'll be a millionaire. Optimistically, he only has eight months to spend it. The decision to liquify his pension was made after his last diagnosis. The cancer had spread through his body quicker than any chemo could catch it.

This new commander made the money payout situation happen. Not by pulling strings, but by knowing the rules inside and out. This new commander is a highly principled man, a stickler. Everything is in accordance with rules and regulations. Everything in its place. Everything and everyone. That's the way things should be.

Seth is putting the last of the magazines into his backpack. It's German and has quite the cover. This little tasty is not only getting made airtight but is jerking two guys off. He looks closer at her hands. Good girl. She knows how to handle cock, and lots of it.

A thought occurs to him. Wright's hands got all fucked up before she joined up with Special Forces. They don't have her new prints on file. They never took new ones. That won't do. This new commander won't care for that. He'll shoot off an email to the commander before he leaves today.

The missing guy's woman knows that Wright is involved. Shawna. She's hot. Tight for a mom. He'd reassured this fuckable mother that they'd get to the bottom of it. Got her busy snooping around.

Besides, why else did the report come on his last day? It's like it's his destiny to sort Wright out. Can't fight destiny. He's going to make sure she remembers exactly who he is—and what he's capable of. Just like yesterday, today is turning out to be an outstanding day. He's excited, alive in every fibre of his being. Tomorrow is his real send-off with the boys at the strippers. It will be glorious.

AFTER ANOTHER RESTLESS day, Christine is in bed texting Joey. She needs his help and is working her way up to asking for it. Joey knows this and makes her do it.

Christine closes her eyes, holding her phone with both hands away from her like she's squishing a stink bug. She pushes send. "I need help."

Joey is not interested in justification, rationalization, conspiracy, or politics. Joey is interested in the truth and nothing but the truth. Once you are speaking the truth, he's all ears.

"What's going on?"

Christine stares at the wall of her bedroom, at the Alex Colville painting of the ravens flying, and wishes she were out there with them.

She takes a deep breath and types, "I'm afraid."

"Of what?"

Christine has spent the last two days trying to talk herself down after the incident with Shawna and the muffins. She has also meditated, tapped, rocked, been grateful, done breath work, and maxed out on her natural downers. You can only drink so much camomile tea. Nothing is working.

She should just text, "Of myself. I've got ugly ideas. I'm plotting. I'm scheming." But she doesn't. "Of what Shawna is up to."

"Why's that?"

He's on to her already. Now Joey may as well be a customer service robot that she is texting with.

Christine has accidentally dumped half a bottle of lavender into the diffuser on her bedside table. It was next to impossible to pour the oil back into the bottle. The oil is already mixed in with the water. She puts the spouted, tear-shaped top onto the base and switches it on.

"Going away."

"Yeah, sure. Next."

Christine is choking. Large amounts of lavender are being spewed into the air. The diffuser is changing from red to green to purple to yellow. Maybe it's not a tear shape, maybe it's a flame. Joey knows her so well. He knows that prison would be a comfortable place for Christine. Just work out, sleep, eat, and fight. Repeat. Probably a lot of unwanted sexual activity mixed in with all of that, however. Not that great in there. Not that great out here either, in the real world. Maybe she should be caged up. The way the food goes onto those trays with all the ridges alone is worth it. She's always felt safe in a cafeteria line. Apparently in prison that's when people come for you. So much for the cafeteria. That's not good. But neither is this. This isn't very good at all.

"What are you really afraid of?"

Christine can't say it. That she is beyond repair and that all this painful, slow, redemptive work is futile. Finishing not one but two degrees. All the step work. All the therapy. All the deep trauma processing. All the somatic stuff. All the prayer and meditation. Not working. None of it is working. It's a joke. She's a joke. The joke's on her.

This is after achieving advanced meditative states, listening to endless growth discourse from every tradition, and spilling her guts in every kind of therapy. Then came the months of a strange kind of convalescence. She was shocked at how physical the process was. There were spells when she was in a kind of paralysis. She could barely eat or take care of herself.

Shamans call what she was trying to do soul recovery. But Christine knows that after all that work, her soul isn't fully recovered. She's just in some kind of weird limbo. It's as if her whole being is trying to upgrade to a new operating system and can't quite handle the new software. She engages all her discipline just to function in society. Joey doesn't seem to suffer like this. No one else seems to suffer like this. How the fuck does she put this in a text?

"Losing control."

"Nice try."

Damn. Christine knows what the real answer is. She cannot type those words. Even to Joey. She will not type them. She will not say that God hates her. That's between her and God. Yes, she is suffering and it's intense, but compared to her past, things are at a dull roar. She doesn't want to make it worse.

Christine types out instead, "Is it wrong to make her look bad?" She doesn't send the text. Letter by letter she erases this stupid question from her phone.

"Condemn her, condemn yourself."

She knows that. The phone chirps again. "And the other way around too."

Christine politely thanks Joey and sends him farm animal emojis. He responds by sending her some fairies and the merman emoji and signs off.

Christine does not feel better. She feels worse. She gives up trying to shut off the light show on the diffuser. After pushing two buttons about thirty times, she leaves it stuck on red.

She plugs her phone in and checks her alarm for the morning. She gets on her knees for the two seconds it takes to say thank you three times to a god that hates her.

Christine can barely breathe and curls up on the side of the bed farthest from the lavender cloud. So this is what it's come to. Lavender is not going to cut it.

A feeling slides in and joins Christine under the covers. A heavy, sedating fog begins to settle in her mind. It's pleasant and familiar. It's powerful. It's nostalgic, and it whispers promises of relief. Christine knows this feeling so well, but not nearly as well as it knows her. It's intoxicating. Christine begins to calm. Her breathing settles.

She pulls the blankets around her. A new plan of action presents itself. A fading part of her mind knows it's false. Says don't trust it. Christine doesn't care. She'll take it. The edges of her mouth begin to curl up ever so slightly. Okay, she won't mess with Shawna. Joey's right. But Joey didn't say anything about that fucking MP.

THE NEXT MORNING, Christine calls the base and asks to be put through to the base commander's office. His secretary's voice-mail message is curt. Christine leaves a message stating that she wishes to make an appointment with the commander.

Her phone rings five minutes later. Christine can come in right away. It is just after eleven. It will be good to take care of this before lunch.

She drives past the Carson Club and makes her way to the naval base. She has not been here for years. Not much has changed. The condominiums continue to stack up and multiply on the outskirts of the base. The main daytime drinking hole burned down a few years back. The yacht club has a new sign.

After showing her identification at the gate and parking the car, she rehearses what she's going to say. She'll express concern about the MP's menacing conduct around frail seniors. And she'll hint about the dangers of poor community relations. Got to be nice to old people. Can't just take a lifetime of taxes out of them and then dispose of them. What kind of society is that? Not our society. This will be easy.

Christine noted Mrs. Dee's reaction to the MP's hard-on. This is not difficult with someone like Mrs. Dee. She's like a mood ring—she changes colour. When faced with that part of the MP pointing straight at her, Mrs. Dee had gone from pink to white.

Then there had been some sort of commotion in the parking lot before the parish supper. When Mrs. Dee was telling of his hot-wheeled exit that spit up gravel, the Sisters sounded off, one after the other.

Sister Karen, who brought Christine Brussels sprouts, ensured her mouth wasn't full when she quietly stated, "That's aggression."

Sister Linda, who brought the sweet potato casserole with candied pecans on top, said mid-chew, "Sounds like somebody was having a little temper tantrum with their car."

And Sister Maria, the oldest and most frail, was up dishing herself a second plate while she called over her shoulder, "What an asshole."

This will be a piece of cake. She needs to throw that MP off her scent. She thought she was done with that sick, fucked up attention directed at her by some of her colleagues. That nauseating mix of titillation with hatred. She can spot it a mile away. He wants to wipe her off the face of the earth, and he'll enjoy doing it. That's the only way he gets his kicks. Little Kassman is probably still a virgin.

In the lobby, she shows her ID at reception. The building is like a lot of buildings constructed in the 1950s and 1960s, with large inner spaces, high ceilings, and minimalist furniture. There are black and white photos of antiquated machinery lining the walls. She stares at a piece of firefighting equipment that looks like a raincoat while the commissionaire checks her face against her ID photo.

She walks down the corridor leading to the commander's office and opens the door that leads into the reception area. She has only just taken in the pale blue walls and the blue rug when her name is called.

An older yet spry man with a stiff upper lip calls for Sergeant Wright. He is a four-ringer, a Navy captain, with the next stop being rear admiral. He is standing in his doorway as she approaches—no handshake on offer. He closes the door behind her and walks her to the middle of his massive office.

"You're out of dress, Sergeant."

The tone is not jovial or friendly. She hasn't worn a uniform in nearly five years, except when she got that damn medal. She is now a civilian. She is not supposed to wear a uniform. She is wearing a collared shirt, suit jacket, and creased slacks.

"Sir?"

The commander sits down neatly at his desk and gives her a laser-sharp look. "What's the problem, Sergeant? Why would you come see your commander dressed like this?"

She remains standing. She will not sit until invited to do so. This is not at all going according to plan.

"Sir, I'm not sure if you are aware, but I'm in a vocational reintegration,"

"I am aware. I am apprised. Are *you* aware that you are still a member in active service until the thirtieth of July?"

"I don't—"

"Is that a yes or a no, Sergeant?"

Fuck. Always mixing up the J months. Fuck. Wasn't it January thirtieth?

"I may have mixed up that date, Sir."

"Mixed it up."

"Sir."

"As in a cocktail, Sergeant? Or do you have a time machine? Mixed it up exactly how? How does one mix up a date?"

"I have no excuse, Sir."

"Indeed, is that so? Well then, are you mixed up about dress regulations?"

"No, Sir."

"So, please tell me what is this issue that you wish to see me about. Aside from your inability to keep dates straight in your head."

His desk is enormous. Light, polished wood. Clean. Except for one file sitting squarely in one corner. There are renderings of naval battles and warships hanging at precisely the same height around the office. The many ribbons on his uniform prove that he's been intensely successful.

"The MP who came to my parish. His conduct was reported to me as offensive and frightening."

"Offensive."

"Yes, Sir."

"Frightening."

"Yes, Sir." Christine feels a bead of sweat run down from an armpit. The commander is so still she wonders if he is breathing.

"Unless he shot someone or ran over somebody, I'm not interested."

"I see."

"You see what, Sergeant?"

"I see, Sir."

"It has come to my attention that your fingerprints are out of date."

"Out of date, Sir?"

"Yes. Stop repeating everything I say. You failed to update your record after your, ah, incident with your hands. Report to base identification and take care of this immediately. Dismissed." He looks over at his computer screen and begins typing.

Christine turns and exits. Only when she is outside does she allow herself to process what has just occurred. Was he waiting for her?

Christine looks down at her hands. They've healed remarkably well. It's not like they didn't have years to sort out her fingerprints. Are they really that different? Why do they want them now?

When she was a new recruit, her supervisor gave her the wrong gloves to pick up hot brass during a massive international manoeuvre. Picking up brass mid-shoot was perfectly safe if you hit the emergency stop and wore the right gloves, except that she wasn't. The gloves melted away on contact, but not completely. Some of the glove melted into the seared edge of her flesh where her fingerprints used to be.

It was when they flew her to the military triage unit in a helicopter that she decided to join Special Forces. No more amateur hour. Time for the right gloves—all the time.

She checks her watch. Almost noon. The base identification office will be closed. The public servants around the base squeeze out about four hours of work a day. The rest is spent complaining, smoking, doing crosswords, and eating. They will definitely not be in.

The entrance to the office is beside one of the commander's windows. She senses that he is watching. She must be seen to make an effort. The office is on the second floor in the building beside cells, the base jail. She barely remembers her one night locked up there. Except that she had pissed off the MP who showed up on Easter.

She moves up the stairs two at a time. She pulls on the handle. It will be locked. It's not. The door flies right open, and to her dismay the wicket is also open. Bored, miserable faces of two disgruntled public servants gaze at her indifferently.

"ID," grunts the big one. A mountain of a man stands up. Probably needs the elevator up to the second floor. His chin, neck, and man-breasts pour onto a huge gut, making his appendages seem smaller than they are. Christine wonders what this one does in a fire drill. Can he reach the alarm?

After showing her ID, Christine puts it away and moves toward another door that leads to the actual fingerprinting room.

"Excuse me." A frail, skinny woman, the other desk attendant, has remained seated.

"Yes?"

"ID. You were already asked. Why are you failing to comply, Sergeant?"

Christine reaches for her ID again and leans over the counter to show it to the woman. She is seated quite far away, so Christine comes up off her feet to extend her arm as far as possible across the desk. They have been waiting for her, obviously.

The woman is too thin, like a skeleton. Heavy-duty grooming takes place in the mornings for her. Bangs have been curled with an iron, then strategically combed and sprayed. Layers of foundation have been applied. She doesn't really need makeup. What she needs is a steak, or maybe an IV. Christine has seen more robust women in intensive care.

It's him, the Commander. Christine didn't even hear the door open behind her. Like an android, he doesn't appear to be breathing. Those with more than three rings get that special officer training at headquarters in Ottawa. After they are finished with them, these officers not only hear everything, they walk through walls. Christine jumps only on the inside. She is surrounded. They're closing in on her.

"Let's go, Sergeant, don't want to hold up Dick and Jane too much longer." He looks at the two behind the counter and adds, "Thank you, folks, this won't go unrewarded. Remember, Friday is my treat at the yacht club."

Jane, the thin one, is shockingly forceful as she grips each of Christine's digits. Christine is pretty much impervious to physical pain, but not to the intent to do harm. Christine's fingers are over-rotated, as if Jane is trying to twist them right off.

So nice that the Commander will treat these two at the yacht club. Christine wonders if the Commander will join them. The idea of them eating together makes Christine dry heave as she washes the ink off with that orange, grainy scrub for mechanics. She swallows hard. She must get rid of that candlestick properly.

She cleaned it well, but they can do things in crime labs. It's best to make it vanish completely. She should have dug Terry in deeper.

She scours away at the dark ink. Maybe the smell of the orange scrub and the sound of running water will create some sort of interference, preventing the Commander from reading her mind. She is sending out a repeating signal that says one thing loud and clear. Guilty, guilty, guilty.

CHRISTINE REMINDS herself on the drive home that she has been in far worse circumstances. In the grand scheme of things, this is a joke. Being charged with manslaughter or murder doesn't even come close to all the other crap she's been through. So why so nervous? She needs to collect herself, pull herself together.

Joey would say that being unsettled is a good thing because she's thawing out and beginning to feel. She would really rather not. Why not stay frozen? Christine yearns for the numbness that ice, with vodka, can bring.

In one period of hospitalization, after her mission in the desert, she was horrified at how robotic she had become. Like the Tin Man. With no tears. She had wanted to thaw then. She wanted messy, gooey, human feelings. Not any more. No thanks.

Joey isn't messy. Joey is totally emotionally intact. Nimble. Flexible. He's taut like a bow, and his arrows shoot straight. Christine's bowstring is loose and flapping in the wind. She can't nock any arrows, so she just throws them, and they don't go far. It's pathetic, and sometimes the wind catches them and they come winging back at her.

She parks and walks toward the back door of the church. Mrs. Dee's little Prius is there, so she must be. The meditation group is in the church hall for their weekly practice. Many meditators have shown up today, to their sangha. Christine counts over twenty bicycles and a few cars. A lot of them walk. Most of them are fit, especially the older ones. She hopes that they've had no problems with the church ladies.

Mrs. Wilson and Mrs. Dee interrupted a few AA meetings by bringing in coffee, tea, and cookies. Ron spoke to Christine about it right away. Mrs. Dee couldn't understand why they preferred to drink that "swill they call coffee," and Mrs. Wilson said that disposable cups were unacceptable. Christine told them both not to enter the church hall during rental periods unless they intended to participate. She quietly enjoyed their indignation. Mrs. Dee the mood ring turned a few different shades of red, with hints of purple. Mrs. Wilson's sharp little owl face, in quick succession, pursed her lips, frowned and grimaced.

Christine makes her way past the hall to check out the progress on the labyrinth. The bricks are still in a pile and so is the fill. She looks closely over Mr. Marshall's grave, scanning for any sort of telltale indications that Mr. Marshall might have company.

Her cellphone vibrates and screeches loudly. An alarm, the emergency broadcast cellphone text alert message. The screeching really penetrates. Is it coming from elsewhere? Where? Christine's eyes return to Mr. Marshall's grave. Fuck. She moves closer to Mr. Marshall's tombstone and hears a faint chirp. Is that a bird? Did Terry just get a fucking text? Can the battery still be going? Isn't two feet of dirt a sufficient sound barrier?

A memory of a mass grave in Afghanistan comes to her. Arms, legs, and heads, with carrion desert shrikes pecking away. She shoves the image away.

Why did she bury his phone in the first place? A kid could find Terry with its sim card, let alone the police. Can't they?

Christine steps onto Mr. Marshall's grave, squatting down, turning her head to one side and then the other. Both eardrums have been blown out on different occasions, which limits her hearing. Her right ear is better than her left, so Christine settles into a low squat with her head twisted up to the left. She closes her eyes and quiets her breathing. The twist feels good, so she places both hands on her knees to get a little torque. She feels herself relax into a deep, low, twisting squat as her phone judders and screeches again.

She springs up. "Fuck! Ahhhhhh!" It's a hamstring cramp. Christine half hops on one leg and gingerly places the back of her thigh onto the rounded tip of Mr. Marshall's tombstone.

She can feel the muscle at first resist the stretch and then release. Ah, the cramp is going, almost gone. Suddenly, the entire situation is funny. Very funny. A deep guttural laugh rushes up through her whole body, pulsing out her mouth. Ha-ha-ha-ha.

She needs to pee, desperately. She's laughing and crying and laughing. Ha-sob-ha-sob. She pulls her leg off the tombstone, plants both feet firmly on the ground, and arches her back, tossing her head back. Christine snaps her head back upright and sees Mrs. Dee peering out at her from the bottom corner of the office window. Eyes wide as saucers and eyebrows raised. She's white as a ghost.

IT IS MOST unbecoming to peep, and Mrs. Dee had no intention of doing so, but it is quite the show the Reverend is putting on outside. All she had wanted to do was simply come in to prepare for the wedding. Is that too much to ask around here? It has been years since they have had an event of this calibre.

Despite all her church has endured, it still exudes a kind of majesty. She was minding her own business, locating the mini-vases to affix on the pews for flowers. It was that piercing wail that brought her attention to this bizarre exhibition. So urgent and close. Could be a new police siren. Leaving her shoes on, she climbed up onto the sofa to take a look-see. And there was Christine, in a most vulgar squat for a graveyard. She looked like an orangutan or gorilla. What on earth? Completely undignified. Then comes some yoga. Heaven knows why women think life's problems are solved by sticking their fannies up in the air in public.

Lord have mercy, she's spotted me! Oh bother, now she's heading this way! Mrs. Dee attempts to hop off the couch as Christine swiftly comes in through the door.

"So glad I caught you, Mrs. Dee! I need your help!" Christine calmly holds a steady, strong arm up to her, helping her step down to the floor. Christine's eyes are wet, and she has the remains of a smirk on her face. Mrs. Dee tugs at her cardigan to straighten it.

What can she say to this? To this audacity? To this undignified behaviour? She can feel her head wobble a little every time she blinks. Why can't people just behave properly? What is this creature? A grave-defiling beast, or a priest? Which is it?

"Yes. I'm looking for the alter candlesticks. You know, the set we used on Easter?"

Well, of course she is. She probably wants to ruin the other one or perhaps scratch her hairy-ape back with it.

"The one was beyond repair, so I gave that set to the Sisters."

The Reverend doesn't care for that at all. Her usual glare is back.

"I see. Well done, Mrs. Dee. It is a shame. About the darkening, I mean."

No more funny business. The Reverend sits down at her desk and begins typing on her keyboard.

Mrs. Dee is reluctant to turn her back on the Reverend, and she begins slowly to back away, toward the door leading into the church. She frantically clutches at the doorknob behind her. Christine looks up and pins her with her implacable stare.

Mrs. Dee gasps.

"Mrs. Dee, there is nothing to be afraid of. It was just a laugh, that's all. Have you never laughed that hard? You should try it, you might like it."

Finally, Mrs. Dee is inside the church, safely out sight of that woman. A refreshing coolness wafts up from the church floor on this very warm day. The smell of wood polish and the sight of crisp linen meet her as she walks over to the sanctuary. Mrs. Dee sighs and feels her blood pressure returning to normal. The Reverend doesn't have any idea what she, Ingrid Dee, enjoys.

The click of Mrs. Dee's shoes, as she walks alone in this, her house of God, is loud in the echoing space. She comes up onto the carpeted stair. This new pile is outstanding, so durable yet luxurious. Hides the wine spills so nicely. She deeply genuflects in front of the reserve sacrament. She is not too old to do that.

Mrs. Dee likes wood polish, perfectly arranged flowers, prayer books and hymn books in order from left to right. She looks at the gleaming stone floor, the rows of pews, and the light pouring in the stained-glass windows in the early afternoon. She takes pleasure in the thought of the wedding coming up tomorrow, the lovely white dress with a flowing train. The orderly beauty of the service.

CHRISTINE'S HAMSTRING is thinking about cramping up again. She doesn't have time for that. She must find that candlestick and deal with Terry's phone. While Mrs. Dee was looking at her like she had two heads, Christine was about to do an internet search for maximum battery lifetimes. Before she pressed enter, she paused. She knows better. The police could easily bring up this search history with a warrant, and most likely without one.

Christine picks up the office phone and calls the Sisters. Sister Leanne, the young novice, answers.

"Hi there, Sister, it's Reverend Wright calling. How are you today?"

"Oh hello, Mother! I am very well today. Very well. What can I do for you?"

Christine cringes a bit at that term of address, even though she is old enough to be Sister Leanne's mother. "I understand that two of our alter candleholders have come into your care?"

"Yes, they did Mother, but I'm afraid they've been sold," Sister Leanne says with a nervous squeak.

"Sold?"

"Yes, Mother. Sold. At our spring rummage sale. We, as you know, desperately need the money. And besides, one of them was, well, beyond repair."

Christine restrains herself. When the insurance was redone on the entire parish it indicated that these items would fetch tens of thousands of dollars on the collector's market. Surely the Sisters knew this? If they were so hurting for money, why didn't they just ask? The candlesticks' origin and lineage alone may have made them almost priceless, and together as a pair, who knows?

"Indeed. I understand completely. I hope they brought a good price. Who did you sell them to?" It is not too late. She will simply explain to the auction house and get the candlesticks returned.

"Twenty-five dollars, Mother! I sold them myself. Cash. They went to a large gentleman. Looked like a lumberjack. Plaid jacket. I didn't catch a name, but he only bartered me down to half price, which I think is something, don't you?"

Christine looks up at the ceiling, takes in a deep breath, holds it, and closes her eyes. She calls for control and it slams down like a guillotine. She uses this technique when faced with unrecoverable casualties while under fire. Now she is using it for church candlesticks.

What the hell is God up to? God and her guardian angel are probably laughing at her right now. Howling. God probably warns, "Don't laugh too hard. I might send you down there again."

"Yes, Sister, that is indeed something. I'm glad you got such a good price."

"Thank you, Mother, and thank you for your generosity. If everyone knew the yield of generosity, they would give and give."

"Isn't that the truth? Thank you for your time, Sister, I will not keep you from your work. God bless you."

"And you, Mother."

Christine hangs up and sets off to walk to the coffee shop down the street. She'll use their internet. Who cares if the sisters gave away thousands of dollars? Really. Who cares? Is this why she was pulled out from hell? To run around like this?

The cherry trees have lined her path with petals. It is warm and cloudless. She yanks her collar off at one of Victoria's five-way intersections, throws her shoulders back, and tries to stand tall as she waits for the pedestrian light. A monkey puzzle tree reaches out its awkward branches, soaking up the warmth.

God cut her loose from hell so that she could live, and live well. Life doesn't have to look like TV or anything, but it would be nice to have a friend, maybe a sense of belonging. Who gives a shit? She doesn't care. This might be as good as it gets, this hellish existence. She'll take it—or maybe not. Maybe she should have just let Terry choke her the fuck out. Just lain there and let him strangle her. No, no good. He probably would have botched it and she'd be in a coma or something.

The pedestrian light tells her to walk, and she begins to stride across the street. There were many times in her life when she could not stride. She forces her legs to drive out from high in her waist, almost from her solar plexus. As she moves, she lets her legs swing out as far as they will go, bringing the other behind. With each step, she tells herself that freedom is pulling her forward as she leaves her past behind. Total fucking bullshit.

Christine inhales deeply. God, it feels good to breathe. What's the worst-case scenario? She killed someone in self-defence. Well, she probably shouldn't have buried him, but facts are facts.

She arrives at the coffee shop, Grounds for Life. The lineup is short, only two people. The café's computer is free. This is good. She takes her place in line. Okay, let's try grounding. Let's get grounded. Christine plants her feet firmly underneath her. She is a mountain, grounded and strong.

The twenty-something guy in front of her turns around. His earlobes are long and droopy. They look like loops of calamari. Only not very tasty. Almost floppy. He says nothing, just glares. Christine doesn't mind, as long as he doesn't touch her.

Then he turns on her, "Ummm seriously, like I'm not comfortable with your heavy breathing behind meee. ... I'm going to ask you to stop or please stand somewhere else, okay? Thanks."

That's right, she forgot. While Christine was learning how to endure torture, civilian youth were learning how to express all the feelings they experience. Every single one. This was encouraged. This was the new quintessence of health, this kind of sociality.

Knowing better than to touch him, she resists tapping him on the shoulder. She belts out in a sticky sweet, piercing, singsong voice, "Um, okay, like I totally get it, but maybe, you know," she shifts to a lower range, "you could put a bag over your head when you come out in public?" She wrinkles her nose up and squints up her eyes into a kind of deranged, cutesy smile.

Everyone could hear her over the gusts of steaming milk from the cappuccino machine behind the counter. Fairly confident she's had the last word, she waits for him to figure out he's next in line. He orders his coffee, then whispers something to the cashier. A long-lobed secret.

Christine orders her coffee. No longer grounded or breathing deeply, she scans the cashier's face to see how she received Long Lobe's complaint. The young woman takes her order and says nothing, not meeting Christine's eyes.

Christine takes the high stool by the bulletin board behind the computer and brings up the browser. The maximum battery life is under twenty hours, so the phone must be like Terry, dead.

"Um, excuse me."

Christine looks up from the screen to find the cashier standing in front of her. The barista has ceased steaming milk and is instead watching, along with the entire café. Long Lobes is peering over a fanzine at her, grinning.

"I'm asking you to leave. Customers have informed me that honestly, they do not feel safe with you here."

"As you wish." Christine guzzles her lukewarm, seven-dollar coffee, clears the browser's history, and leaves.

Back at the crosswalk, the monkey puzzle tree looks like it's pointing and having a laugh. A shudder passes through her as she hits the button for the pedestrian light. The nerves running down Christine's arms and hands flash as she imagines choking out Long Lobes. She hears him whimper and her responses. "Nighty-night. Shhh. That's right. I know. I know. Shhhhhh. Won't be long now." She imagines the look on all the coffee-drinkers' faces. What would the snooty cashier have to say then?

Christine snaps out of it. Okay, that's enough. Calm down. Get your act together. This is undignified and sinful. Apologize to God and carry on.

Her whole life, Christine has mounted an outstanding front. Despite this, when she crosses the road again, inside she slouches. Always the outsider. It's amazing how much it hurts.

Just forget about it. Get back to the parish, check on the labyrinth, and finish preparations for the wedding tomorrow. Larry has been dragging his feet, promising her "next week" over and over again for a couple of months now. She doesn't know the bride or groom very well, and all attempts to get to know them have been thwarted. The church is just the venue. She is the hired hand, that point was made clear. She expects this kind of thing, and it doesn't really bother her. The church ladies, of course, were delighted with the booking.

The sermon is ready, leaflets printed, ushers briefed, piano player hired. Everything is ready to go except the labyrinth. Right now, it's still just a pile of dirt and bricks.

A block away from the church, Shawna is coming toward her, pushing Terrine in a bright pink stroller. Shawna stiffens and scowls at the sight of Christine's fake-friendly smile.

Lord, help me. What should I do now? Christine feels her shoulders come down. It's too funny—Shawna has her legs spread, braced, as if Christine might be about to tackle her.

"I need to see your office. Forgot something," Shawna says when Christine is within talking distance. Shawna's lips are pressed flat, eyes narrowed.

"Sure, okay." Christine keeps her voice light.

Shawna's phone shoots out of her hand and lands at Christine's feet. Whoopsie. What have we here? A red dot floats on the screen. Christine tries to read the text as she hands it back.

"Thanks."

Great. It's a phone finding app. Looks like the dot you see when you're trying to get somewhere. Like follow the path to the dot.

Christine, Shawna, and Terrine move toward the office entrance. Mrs. Dee meets them on their way and positions herself to block their path. Christine looks past Mrs. Dee and can see Larry leaning against his backhoe by the shed, holding a very expensive-looking imaging device.

"Reverend, Larry needs your permission to x-ray the graves or some such thing."

"Sonic image!" Larry shouts. "Don't want to hit any pipes!"

"I'll just let myself in, Reverend. Mrs. Dee can let me in." Shawna's hands are tight fists.

"Wait. Everyone wait."

"Wait for what?" Mrs. Dee is tapping her foot. Everyone is looking at her.

"No." Christine states.

Shawna doesn't like that word. "No?"

"No, Shawna, today is not a good day. No, Larry, you won't be imaging the grounds."

"But he must," Mrs. Dee flutters. "What if he hits a pipe? What then?"

"I'll just be a minute, Reverend. I really need to get in there." Shawna's usually pale face is pink.

Larry moans, "I don't have all day! Do you want this labyrinth done or not?"

Mrs. Dee joins up with Larry. "Do try to remember it's the Bluefield's wedding tomorrow. I think, if I am remembering correctly, we said there would a labyrinth, isn't that so?"

"Right. I see. Well, let's see if I can be a little more clear for everyone." Christine stands with her hands on her hips. "Shawna, your presence is no longer welcome here, please leave. Larry, we won't be needing you."

"The council decided that I was to do the work!"

Christine looks over at Larry. "That decision has been changed as of now. You will instead take your backhoe and imaging equipment and leave immediately."

Christine looks over at Shawna. "Shawna, why are you still here?"

Mrs. Dee shrugs and begins to help Shawna turn the stroller around in the narrow path.

Christine quickly moves past them, unlocks the office door, steps in, spins around, and slams the door and locks it. Hearing the heavy lock click, Christine thinks to herself that finally Mrs. Dee should be happy about something. The door is locked.

MRS. DEE IS STUPEFIED. That wedding tomorrow is of the utmost importance, and she wants the labyrinth done. Although she appreciates backbone, now really isn't the time. The Reverend's behaviour is becoming increasingly strange.

She watches Shawna storm off toward downtown. Really, you shouldn't push a stroller that fast. Larry is still leaning against his backhoe. She shrugs in his direction. He shrugs back, then gets into the machine and starts it up. It roars off across the residence parking lot and exits onto Yates. A busy road for a backhoe.

Larry is, of course, overcharging the parish, as usual. What would he know about the council anyway? He hasn't attended a council meeting in years. If he had, he'd know just how important this labyrinth is. The Bluefields and Stipenheinds are two of the most prominent families in the area. The stones should have been laid down weeks ago and the whole thing seeded so that it would be a proper garden labyrinth by now.

She leans against the office door. Really, she feels quite weepy. And that young woman, Shawna. She most definitely has a cruel streak in her. Anyone can easily see it in the way she is with her child. What did she want in the office anyway? Could it be that Shawna had something to do with the rug disappearing? And that business with her husband. Not her husband—that's not the right term. People don't use that term. It has also gone out of fashion. Her baby daddy. That business with her baby daddy.

Mrs. Dee surveys the pile of soil that Larry has left behind. Some of it has spilled on Mr. Marshall's grave. That will also have to be fixed. There is lots of work that needs to be done today. They need to come up with a plan.

Mrs. Dee unlocks the office door. The doorknob will not turn. Obviously, the Reverend is holding it on the other side of the door.

"Reverend?"

"Yes, thank you so much, Mrs. Dee. I'll see you Sunday."

"But what about the wedding tomorrow? The labyrinth?"

"Oh, don't you worry about that. I have it in hand."

"I don't see how."

"Don't you worry. I'll see you Sunday." Her tone is final.

"Did you see that cellphone?"

"What?"

"I found it under your couch, I've placed it on your desk. It's dead."

"I see it. Thank you."

Mrs. Dee releases the door knob. If this strange woman wants to ruin the wedding of the season, she can be my guest. This was their chance to become a part of the life of the community again. Maybe she should just go read to Norman. She isn't invited to the wedding anyway.

"Very well, Reverend, see you Sunday."

CHRISTINE LETS GO of the doorknob and slumps onto the couch. She pulls out her phone and sends a one-word text to Joey.

"Help."

Joey will come through for her despite it being games night for him. It won't be until after the meal and at least one game. This is a monthly thing at his house. Christine has not been invited over to Joey's. Nor is she likely ever to be. Their relationship isn't like that.

Christine decides to build the labyrinth, using the dwindling daylight she can see out the window facing the graveyard. How hard can it be? It's like drawing a hopscotch pattern at the playground. Rocks and dirt. She's parachuted from high altitudes. She's communicated coded coordinates while under enemy fire. She can put a puzzle on top of dirt. Get a grip.

She opens a drawer in her desk and pulls out the paper labyrinth pattern. The council chose a simplified version of the Notre-Dame de Chartres pattern. Seven circuits. Should be easy. All will be well.

Christine steps out into the cooling evening. There's a little wind, and the leaves of the big madrones at the back of the graveyard are rustling. She will start in the middle of the labyrinth and work outwards.

She makes her way through the pile of bricks to find the right configuration for the centre. Some of the bricks are curved, others aren't. The bricks are nice. They look like cut limestone, but they are really cured concrete.

The instructions recommend transposing the pattern to the

ground with string and sticks. No time for that now. She left the instructions in the office. That's where they'll stay.

She'll half bury the bricks, level with some sand and soil, and seed the whole thing with the grass seed. The whole thing should take two or three hours, tops. Christine eyeballs where the first brick needs to go and then walks to the shed to get the proper tools. She chooses a heavy, sharp pick. This time she'll let the tool do the work, no holding back for fear of hitting something. The area is clear of any graves.

Christine returns to the centre of the imagined labyrinth. The whole thing will be about fifty feet across, with the centre being about halfway down the length of the church, just before the transept. An axis away from the parking lot connecting the church, graveyard, and hall. It will be nice.

She raises the pick high and lets it fall, her shoulders relaxed. The pick's sharp tip plunges deep into the ground. She hears metal striking metal, and dirt flies into her face. Her eyes have grit in them, and now a high-pressure stream of water is drilling into her face. Christine shrieks and staggers back, sits blindly down on the ground, and rubs at her eyes with a corner of her sleeve.

Holy shit. She's hit a water pipe. Through her murky vision, she sees Joey paying his taxi driver. He's very drunk and wanders toward Christine, passing under the forty-foot arc of water coming from the centre of the labyrinth.

"Powerful. Good water pressure here."

"I know. We gotta get it shut off."

"Girl, you are too much."

"Thanks for coming, Joey."

"I'm gunna help you."

"How was game night?"

"Great, 'cept for trying to throw a Monopoly game to get here faster. Ever tried that? Clue would've been better, cuz we both know how that one ended." Joey giggles and points up at the steady, high stream of water. "What's up with that?"

"I hit a water pipe."

"Just now?"

"Just now."

"Awww, you shouldn't have. Just for me? It's kind of pretty, don't ya think?"

Christine gets up. They both stand in silence, looking at the gusher. "Yeah, Joey. Pretty."

Joey attempts to force the beaming smile from his face. He jumps both feet together and salutes her. "What's the mission, Ma'am?"

"This labyrinth."

"Why?"

"The Bluefield wedding is tomorrow."

"Aren't they paying you, like, fifty bucks?"

"I know, I know."

Joey bends back, almost tipping over as he admires the stream of water. "Roger Dodger, Captain, or should I say aye aye? First order of business is mending that pipe. Then we lay brick!"

Joey breaks into a modified version of the Village People's "YMCA" involving pipe and brick. Christine begins looking around the back of the shed for the shut-off valve behind the mature blackberry bushes. She can't see anything. Rubbing her eyes again, she notices residual ink from her fingerprinting. That and the dirt really showcase the freaky patchwork scarring on her fingers.

It's dusk, and shadows begin to engulf all that is already dark. Night is settling around them. Christine sticks her hand into random spots in the bushes, groping around for the valve. Thorns tear at her skin, and she feels the darkness within her get up from where it was sleeping. Rest time is over.

"TOMMY, WOULD YOU like to share tonight?" Ron always calls him Tommy. Tom likes it. Well, he likes everything about Ron, his sponsor. Big meeting tonight. It's been a week since Terry, his sponsee, went missing. He was hoping to find out some information on where the hell he's disappeared to.

He doesn't even know if that term applies—sponsee. Terry never calls him, but Terry did ask Tom to sponsor him, and Tom agreed. That's what he's supposed to do. He's supposed to reach out a hand to the still-suffering alcoholic or addict. And he's supposed to share when asked, whether he feels like it or not.

He didn't feel like it when he first got started. That's for sure. Last place on earth a person wants to be. But he'll keep going. Ron was there at the door, gave him a big greeting for his first meeting. Ron understands the hell of addiction. And Ron beat it. Stick with the winners.

"Thanks, Ron. Yeah, I'll share. I'm Tom and I'm an alcoholic and addict." Tom glances over to the chalkboard to see what the topics are.

"Uh, okay, the topics are gratitude, step two, and anonymity. All right, I can speak about that." He quickly scans the room, trying to make eye contact. He spots a few doing what he used to do, nibbling on the small disposable cups nervously, like mice. All the AA paraphernalia is out. An ugly burl clock with "One Day at a Time" written around it. A framed, cross-stitched Serenity Prayer propped up against the coffee tin for collections for those recovering while incarcerated. The room is full but is quiet now, as the twenty or so men and women wait for what Tom is going to say.

"I'm grateful for this program. That's for sure. I, uh … Well, I knew something was wrong with me right away. There was nothing social about the way I drank or used. Other people were having fun, not me. I was doing something else. My homeboys, they used to tell me, Tom, you're not partying. You're doing something else.

"My auntie died an alcoholic death. Painful and undignified. People didn't know what to say because she did it to herself. She couldn't stop. I couldn't stop either. I had to drink. At first, I drank to fit in, to feel okay. Then I drank when I was happy. Then I drank when I was in pain. I drank with other people, and I drank alone. I just always had to drink. Then I found cocaine. It let me drink more. And the real me dissolved.

"I used to jack cars down in California. My job was to make them new and get them different plates. But sometimes my job was to tap on the glass, letting whoever was inside know that they needed to get out their car because we were going to take it. Guess what I tapped on the glass with? Scaring moms and dads and everyone. That was me. Pulling people out of their cars at gunpoint.

"The wife left, took my baby girl. House went away. Everything went away. But the drugs and alcohol stayed. In the end, it was just me and them. Until this program. This program introduced me to a power greater than myself that, just like step two says to us, could return me to sanity." Tom nods in the direction of the banners hanging on the wall that state the twelve steps and traditions of Alcoholics Anonymous.

Tom shifts in his chair. The padding had given up long ago. These chairs and meetings are not about being comfortable. Nobody wants to be here. But they need to be here. Tom's back aches. That pain is nothing compared to the hollowing-out, corrosive pain of addiction. Tom sighs.

"And anonymity? Well, that's in tradition twelve. Anonymity is the spiritual foundation of everything. So I asked my sponsor," Tom nods over to Ron. "I asked him, why? Why is anonymity the spiritual foundation of the program? That sounded really important to me. He told me that anonymity as a spiritual principle goes really deep and wide, but that he likes to keep it simple. He told me that he likes to gossip and that he can kick up quite a storm with it. They had to call an ambulance once at his apartment building because of one of those gossip wars. So he told me, tradition twelve for him just means not gossiping.

"I hung the phone up that night for the first time with some hope. I had ninety days sober at that point, but I was a complete mess. I would scream at myself and punch myself in the ribs to fight off the cravings. I probably should have been hospitalized, but I'm afraid of hospitals, as many of us are." Tom sees a few guys nod, a couple of tired-looking women too. "I had hope because finally this was something I could do. I mean, I couldn't do steps one, two, or three. I couldn't do anything, but I could shut my mouth. So I did. I shut it at my job, with my family, and I never tell anyone anything that I hear in these rooms. And five years later, I understand how powerful this anonymity is."

The message is landing on a few of them. But some are still sporting the "bar-star look." Along with the telltale puffiness and discoloration that failing livers bring on, their defensiveness is also visible. Too cool for school. Too cool to live. That's what that ego does. The steps beat the ego out of him, with a two-by-four.

"So, I'll conclude by thanking all of you for being a part of my recovery, because that's how it works for me. I keep working the steps, and coming here and seeing all of you."

After they all recite the Serenity Prayer, he tries to help a really sweet old-timer lady in the kitchen, where she's washing out the coffee urn.

"Tom, you're a good boy. You're not a thug. You're a good boy. God didn't want that for you. You see? You just keep walking the walk, Tom."

"Thanks, Linda. You want help?"

"No, the warm water feels good on my arthritis, Tom. You go have a smoke."

Tom steps outside and finds his boys all gathered around Ron. Tom vapes now. No more cigarettes. Ron is in his glory and speaking full on twelve-step to the boys, the language of a new life. Ron beams with happiness. The street light picks up his shock of silver hair and icy blue eyes.

Ron sniffs the air. "What's the flavour tonight, Tommy?"

"I think they call this one Surfer Pie or something. It's max strength for nicotine."

"Surfer Pie, eh? You go ahead and surf that pie, Tommy. Now, what about Terry? You heard from him?"

Tom shakes his head.

"You know that newcomers have broken fingers, right Tommy? They can't pick up the phone, let alone dial. It's okay if you call him—you go ahead and call Terry."

"He's missing, Ron."

"Missing?"

"Yeah, the police came to the church on Sunday. Took Shawna in for a formal statement. He's been missing since Friday, apparently. I wasn't here last Friday, were you?"

Ron frowns. "Yeah, that's right, I was chairing."

"Terry was here." Sean, who has eight years sober, spoke. "He was a right shitshow. High. Angry. Freaking out about Shawna and the kid. Took over the meeting with his ranting and pacing, scared everyone, and then left. Said he was gonna get rid of the ball and chain for good. Ron went after him."

Tom shakes his head, then turns to Ron. "Did you catch up with him?"

Ron looks uneasy. "Yeah. Yeah, I did."

"Well?"

"I told him not to go home. I told him to go see Christine. And then to call you after. He went. He went to go see her. I watched him go into the church. You know, that back door over there."

"Hmm." Tom takes another long drag off his vape. From what he gathered, Christine hadn't seen Terry Friday night

"Don't worry, Tommy, she's built for … for the likes of him."

"Right."

"Right." Right, the murmur goes around the group. It's quiet for a moment while everyone looks away, blowing smoke.

At home, Tom tries Terry's cell a few times. No answer. Then he calls his landline. Shawna answers, and she wants him to come over.

"It's not too late?"

"No, I just got the baby down. I want to talk to you."

When Shawna answers the door, she looks much better than on Sunday. Man, she's intense. He feels the pull of those clear, doll-like eyes, which distract from the mean mouth.

"Come in, Tom, come and sit down. Don't bother taking your shoes off. Do you want a coffee?"

Tom takes his shoes off anyway and takes a chair at the kitchen table. "No thanks, Shawna. Maybe a glass of water?"

"Sure, okay." Shawna turns and opens a cupboard. She looks for a clean glass amid all the plastic. There's a stack of disposable cellphones in the cupboard, unopened. Shawna closes the cupboard with the glass in her hand and opens the fridge to reveal a bunch of wilted kale beside a smudged pitcher of water. She fills the glass and then checks the freezer for ice. Tom notices two bottles with red caps—forties it looks like.

"Sorry, there's no ice." Shawna pulls up a chair across from him.

"No problem. Rum?"

"I thought you were sober." She does this exaggerated head tilt. "I mean, you are Terry's sponsor."

"No, I mean in the freezer. Is that rum?"

Shawna twists in her chair, as if to look at the fridge, her slinky blouse and pants hugging her shapely body. Tom can feel the pull growing stronger inside him. Ron told him that this is codependency. It's not the same as real attraction. It's unhealthy, and he's supposed to be really careful about it.

"No, that's moonshine. It's Terry's. His uncle or something has a still on the prairies. It just shows up. Along with other stuff."

Tom puts a hand on his water glass. "So is Terry still drinking?"

"Oh yeah. Big time. He never quit. Same with the blow."

"Helps him drink more."

"Yep." She sneers. "I made him go to the meetings. Go get help."

"How?"

"At first, I told him that I would leave if he didn't. This was right after Terrine was born."

Tom feels for Terry. It's useless for a real addict to try to clean up like that. With tough love or threats. They don't work.

"And then I could tell that wasn't enough." She's scowling now. This girl is getting her hate on—it's like it's holding her upright in her chair.

KATHERINE WALKER

Tom takes a sip of water. "That must have been hard."

She looks momentarily puzzled. "No, I just told him if he didn't go, I would rat him out."

Tom breaks eye contact and looks at his glass. There is something floating in the water. The fake woodgrain from the table is magnified through the glass. His hands are sweating. He can feel the sweat interacting with whatever is on the table surface. He should leave.

Shawna shifts in her seat. She is waiting for a response. Tom moves his glass around. Don't drink it. Get out. Don't find out more. Get out. Ron's raspy voice is in his head. "Danger. Time to go, Tommy. The house is on fire, Tommy."

Tom stands up. "Well, it's getting late. I'm going to get going."

"I didn't. I didn't rat him out."

"Okay, well, it's none of my business."

"Well, I did, but then I cancelled it. I called them back and I took it back. Those guys just act tough. They're nothing. They're clowns."

Tom is new to Canada but he knows the mob, he knows gangs. They don't take cancellations. And if they are clowns, they're not very funny. You don't want to hear them laughing.

Shawna is on her feet, moving to the door. Tom makes sure he gets there first. He fumbles a little with the screen door and then he's out. Thank God.

"You're Terry's sponsor. That makes it your business. Listen, I think that Reverend is hiding him or something. You and her are close, right? Can you find out?" Shawna's voice is piercing. She lingers on the step as Tom hustles to his car, and in a flash, she's in the street, in front of his car door.

He stands there, unable to open his door with her in the way. "Uh," he says.

106

"Is that a yes?" She's practically jumping up and down she's bouncing so nervously on her feet.

"Yes, we're close. I'll, uh ... I've got to go, Shawna."

She smiles and leans toward him.

Oh God, she wants a hug. He gives in and lets her hug him. He's got to get out of here. She pushes her breasts into him. She smells like nail polish remover.

He waits until he is at a red light to call Ron.

"Tommy."

"Hey, Ron. So I just left Shawna's, and uh ..."

"And uh what, Tommy? Spit it out."

"She's dangerous. That's a dangerous woman." The red traffic light glows like a warning. The phone has handed over to the car's hands-free system.

"Well, what the hell were you doing over there?"

"I know, I know."

"What do you know, Tommy? Let me guess. You were going to rescue her? Hey, let me ask you, did you ride over there on a white horse?"

"Well ..."

"Well, nothing! Baby momma to a drug dealer? I just regret sending him over to Christine's the other night. You just steer clear. Hear me? Tommy!"

Tom is shocked at Ron's tone. "Yes, yes, I hear you, Ron." Tom can see that stack of disposable cells in Shawna's cupboard. Terry must have been in deep if he had to hide his tracks like that.

"Hey, come on now. Relax. What's the last thing a codependent sees before they die?"

"I don't know, Ron. What?"

"Someone else's life flashing before their eyes." Hoarse laughter fills the car. Tom begins to wonder when this light is going to turn and looks up. He notices a spider dangling from the visor. Hanging from a single thread. Ron's going on about boundaries, detachment, and one step at a time. Tom pulls the thread from the visor. He unrolls the window and tries to drop the spider outside.

Now the spider is crawling up his arm. He takes aim to give it a flick as the light turns green and the car behind him honks. He doesn't care. Let him honk. He's got to get rid of this thing.

"THOSE WHOM GOD has joined together, let no one pull apart."
The words are asunder, but no one wants to hear that. Asunder.
Christine lifts her arms to bless and present the husband and wife
to the congregation. She is struggling to keep her hands up high.
Her shoulder is screaming. She gave up on finding the cut-off last
night and repaired the leak with rags, electrical tape, and clamps
she found in the shed. Joey passed out, and she threw the labyrinth together herself.

Despite her two hours of sleep, the wedding really has gone
well, and they've made it to the grand finale. The piano player is
ready. Christine does the blessing, the couple turn and face the
congregation, and she pronounces them husband and wife, which
is the cue for the piano player to begin the recessional hymn.

There's the sound of breaking glass. All heads swivel toward
the stained-glass window with the missionary in it, and … there's
water coming through a fist-sized hole. The shattering glass didn't
hit anyone, and thankfully, the water broadens from a narrow,
powerful stream to a spray. The spray still has some pressure
behind it. Christine feels some on her face, and it wakes her up a
bit. The groom's family is getting rained on, but only a little. The
bride turns back around to face Christine, and she looks pissed
off. The front of her dress is a bit wet, but above the grimace, her
mascara is fine.

"My dress," the bride hisses and whips back around. Christine
reaches for the bride's train to get it out of her way. Christine is not
quick enough, and the bride steps down and immediately trips.

Her new husband catches her from falling, but not the tiara. More gasps as the tiara falls to the ground. It wobbles right through a little puddle by the groom's father's feet and over to the bride's side of the gathering.

The piano player finally begins. Christine is the only one singing. The bride's mother picks up the tiara. Instead of placing it back on her daughter's head, she quickly tucks it behind her back and also begins singing. The rest of the people start singing, and the procession out of the church begins.

Christine walks behind the bride and groom. She doesn't know a single person in the church right now, including the piano player, who will be paid thirty out of her fifty dollars. Christine just wants to get this day over with.

The couple turned down her offer of premarital counselling and reminded Christine that the bride's ancestors are buried in the church's graveyard. They had both grown hostile when Christine asked if they had been baptized. Christine gets it, the distaste for the church. But still, it's not like she asked them if they eat kittens or anything.

The bride's train is leaving a wet, muddy smear on the floor behind her. Sort of like a slug. Christine just looks down and follows the smear. Don't smile. Don't smirk.

The wedding party makes it to the exit without further incident and forms a receiving line. She takes her spot beside them outside.

Christine takes her place at the edge of the labyrinth, or the muddy abomination that she worked on until four a.m. It is remarkably ugly. She buried Terry's cellphone in it after smashing it with the pick. That was the highlight of her Friday night.

The bride's mother steps in front of her.

"No organ? The piano was a … um … pleasant surprise." She wrinkles her nose.

"No, Mrs. Stipenheind, it needs some repairs."

"I see. Well, these things do happen. I think we'll forgo the photos in the labyrinth. Get off to the club right away." Mrs. Stipenheind begins walking toward the labyrinth and then rushes back.

"Well, now we know where that water came from. I think you have a problem, Reverend, that needs your attention."

The scowling bride and groom with a glance excuse Christine from the receiving line.

"May your days together be a source of strength. God bless both of you." Christine gives her best send-off smile and makes her way toward the labyrinth. Maybe she should tell them she likes her kittens extra crispy.

The centre point of the labyrinth is now a bubbling mud pool. Some of the bricks have come loose. The entire area is flooding and water is seeping toward the graveyard and church. Christine will have to take a trip to the hardware store right away and fix the pipe properly. She can't have the water utility digging around.

The piano player comes to find her, looking for his money.

"Water must have come right through the glass. What a shame."

"Yes, that window had a crack in it." Christine hands him his envelope and waits for all the guests to leave. It doesn't take long. Someone has thrown rice. Mrs. Dee will be very unhappy about that, and the mud, and the window. As soon as Christine fixes the pipe, she'll clean the church. Vacuum up the rice. Mrs. Dee would have a heart attack if she saw this mess.

Christine makes her way up to the broken window to inspect the damage, careful not to step on any graves. All the windows must have been done at the same time because the faces are repeated and so is the hair. In the ones Jesus is in, he looks bored, with an expression that says, "Thanks anyways, Humanity, but you missed the point—I'm bored with you, and I'm not coming back."

The missionary window depicted a shirtless Indigenous man kneeling in front of a priest. Complete with stereotypical head-dress. The bright colours and cookie-cutter shapes made the window look like a cartoon, fabricating a sense of innocence into a scene that is anything but. Now there is a jagged hole where the kneeling man's head and the priest's crotch were. Looks like the priest is trying to subdue an explosion in the area of his gonads.

Twenty minutes later, Christine goes to the hardware store. Incredibly fatigued, she makes her way through the vast emporium that offers a fix for almost every problem. Not her problem. Her problem is that she is alone in the world and God is testing her. Is this how Noah felt? Jonah? Okay, let's not get ridiculous. There was a water pipe leak. Just find the right clamp and get out of here.

THE NEXT WEEK Mrs. Dee is driving to the garden centre. She is determined to stay far away from the Reverend, the broken window, and that monstrosity some may choose to call a labyrinth. The grounds of the church are now completely ruined with that uneven and dangerous mud heap. The Reverend did not level the sand first, and had, in her astute wisdom, placed it on top of the soil. Nothing will grow in that.

Mrs. Dee just hopes that the garden centre will, in fact, allow her to return the second shipment of ecograss for a refund. She explained everything when she cancelled the delivery, but they still sent out the invoice. After all the years of business she has brought them and sent their way. Ecograss is very pricey. Very pricey indeed.

Mrs. Wilson told her all about the Bluefield wedding—she had it first-hand from one of the guests. Scandalous. They'll be lucky if they ever see another wedding at the church. People can and do sue over things like that!

She walks to the back of the store, where she knows she'll find the manager. After showing her the invoice, the manager puts up her hands.

"The best we can offer is credit, Mrs. Dee. I'm sorry."

"I see. Well, that's just fine. I'd like the same in value in the songbird mix birdseed. Have them take it to my car."

"That's a LOT of birdseed."

"Yes. Indeed it is. Does it have sunflower?"

"Let me check. No, it doesn't."

"That should be suitable. Also, I need a few hornet's nest spray-can things. You know, that fill the nest with foam, killing everyone inside?"

To protect Norman, Mrs. Dee continues to wear a mask when in stores. Being unable to see the mouth makes moments like this so much easier. The mouth conveys a lot of information, even when shut.

"Yes, of course. Right away, Mrs. Dee."

Driving back to the church, Mrs. Dee's usually jabbering brain is oddly silent. She feels like she is embarking on a grand adventure. If the Reverend thinks she has the market cornered on causing chaos, well, she has another thing coming.

Regardless, there is still work to be done. It is high time to get rid of that wasp nest behind the church hall. If you leave these kinds of things too long, they can turn into real problems. The front of the hall looks civilized, but the back is a different story. Same with the residence. Larry is supposed to be going in there from time to time to do heavy pruning, which he never does.

Mrs. Dee stops off at home to put on her safari clothes. She'll need them. Driving over to the church, she keeps checking in the rear-view mirror, looking at the bags of birdseed. Perfectly delightful. That'll keep things exciting, won't it? The Reverend said she needed a laugh. Well, she is going to have one. She is going to have a nice, big laugh.

She slowly walks toward the wasp nests at the back of the church hall. Normally, Larry takes care of this kind of job, but since he was sent packing, it's doubtful this nest will ever get dealt with. This thick brush behind the hall is such a wilderness. The overgrowth has started to engulf the red brick wall at the back, where the bushes are thick and strong and have steadily over the years reclaimed their place in the scheme of things. She enjoys

114

this kind of task, but must be careful. Some of those thorns could go right through you.

The parish grounds are nestled beside a park. That's why the developers all these years have licked their lips. Some years back, a developer joined Church Council. Mrs. Dee smelled her from a distance.

Now Mrs. Dee is armed with three cans of "Nest-Blaster" in a canvas bag. She has fitted up her safari hat with some netting. All her skin is covered. She hears the wasps. Their buzzing is loud, almost ferocious. Mrs. Dee cautiously moves closer. The buzzing subsides slightly. They know she is nearby. Do they know what she has planned? Do they know what these cans of "Nest-Blaster" mean for them?

This is a most unsavoury business, but she doesn't make the rules. These wasps are finishing off the bees that humanity hasn't yet managed to kill off. Larry never listens to her—this could have been avoided if the spring queens had just been taken care of.

She spots the nest that is right by the back door. The colour of the surrounding tree bark, the papery orb is fastened along the branch of a maple. She'll have to use the steps to get to the nest, and she hasn't thought to bring a ladder.

She is about to lower her netting when she spots a young man inside the back of the hall in the kitchen, pouring himself some water. He doesn't have a shirt on. God knows what group is in there now. She is not allowed in the hall any longer. Forbidden from her own church hall! He spots her, and his face lights up. He flings open the back door. The door scrapes past some brambles, with thorns scratching at the paint.

"Ingrid!"

Mrs. Dee nearly falls back into the thorns. He has a bed sheet draped around his waist. Behind him on the kitchen counter, she glimpses what looks like a fruit platter. A few wasps hover in the doorway, then dart right past his face toward it.

He reaches out, taking her hand, and pulls her quickly up the rickety steps and inside.

"I can't come in here."

"Of course you can, Ingrid! This is your place!" He closes the door behind her. Branches press up against the windows. The kitchen now feels like a fort, the kind she made with her brother out of blankets draped over chairs.

"You know my first name." She nervously eyes the wasps circling the platter. "I do not know you."

He turns to the fruit platter, waves the wasps off, and calls to the group gathered in the main hall. "Careful! Some wasps came in the back door!"

People are setting up easels and chairs. Mrs. Dee spots charcoal sticks, conté crayons, and pencils. All of which she used in what seems like another life that is not her own. All the artists are gathered around a raised platform for the model. That must be for him, this young man.

"This time of year is so perfect. For the light, to draw, don't you think, Ingrid?" He is now handing her a very ripe, dripping piece of pineapple. No plate, no napkin.

Seized by recklessness, Mrs. Dee takes the slippery fruit from his bare hand and puts it in her mouth.

The juices have dripped onto the floor. Mrs. Dee looks down to see drips on the bed sheet. She sees one of his bare feet. The intense flavour makes her palate ache.

With a juicy full mouth, she mumbles, "Young man, what is your name?"

He looks perplexed. "I'm Dominique Wilson's great-nephew, Evan."

"I see, Evan." She held him as a baby. Twenty-odd years ago.

He is now bending toward the counter, sliding a long piece of pineapple off the platter for himself. He opens his mouth and slips the pineapple in, and droplets of juice land on Mrs. Dee's blouse.

Evan makes a face with his mouth full. "So sorry! Let's go draw, shall we?"

"I can't!"

"You can, I know you can. Auntie Dominique told me you can."

"Well, yes, that may be. But I don't have pencils or paper!"

"Use mine. I have the best." He has somehow ushered her out of the kitchen. No eyebrows are raised as Evan sets up a chair and easel and opens his toolbox full of art supplies. He takes one last look at his watch before taking it off, dropping the bed sheet to the floor, and jumping up to the platform.

Evan strikes a few poses in quick succession—this young man is a bit of a ham—and this garners a few chuckles. The goal is to maintain stillness of course, so he settles down into a wide-legged stance. He arches his back slightly and puts his hands up, keeping his elbows tucked in. It is like someone is throwing him a beach ball. Or he's having a jolly laugh.

"You sure?" the instructor asks.

"Yes. The five-minute quick draws, right? To warm up?"

"Yes, five minutes."

A few adjust their chairs, but there really is no time for that. Mrs. Dee picks up a piece of charcoal with her sticky fingers and makes a few strokes on the paper.

Mrs. Dee feels the channels in her perception adjust. She recalls that she is an instrument influenced entirely by the light falling through the hall windows. The spectrum that shapes Evan shapes all, and is demanding a response from her.

"Excuse me, so sorry." A gentle voice from behind. Mrs. Dee turns around to see a man her own age pointing to his head. Mrs. Dee reaches up to touch the bee netting. It is quite voluminous when folded back like that.

"Oh dear." She quickly removes her safari hat and returns to her drawing. Her hand moves the charcoal over the paper. Her strong fingers smudge the lines between being and not being. Evan takes form quickly on the heavy, luxurious paper. He is beautiful.

Mrs. Dee tells herself this is not what she came for. The wasp nest will have to wait. They know that she is busy elsewhere. She hears them as they buzz about the platter in the kitchen, undisturbed, feasting on the very ripe fruit.

CHRISTINE IS CATCHING UP on the office work piled on her desk. Attendance has been steadily increasing over the summer, and now all sorts of people are here on end-of-July Sundays. Christine isn't sure why.

First, the earthy women showed up, perfumed with patchouli, wearing long, colourful skirts and sandals, their armpits unshaven. Then came their male counterparts, earthy men, sporting wisdom buns, sandals and the occasional sarong. Next were twenty-somethings with the latest hair. Iridescent white, shimmery purple, and rainbow-coloured locks began to populate the back rows. Then came some people with money. Subdued, quality, and designer clothing began to congregate in the middle rows of pews. The rich came in groups, travelling in formation like Canada geese. The newcomers would not encroach on the front row. There was an unspoken rule that the front was left for Mrs. Wilson, Mr. Fowler, and Mrs. Dee—the pillars of the church.

Sometimes the earthy types would seek out guidance, and it was good to see the pillars welcome them, explaining the liturgy. Over the weeks of summer, the church ladies and Mr. Fowler oriented everyone. Mrs. Dee loved to show the newcomers the prayer books, while Mrs. Wilson demonstrated genuflection, and Mr. Fowler expounded, rather too loudly, about the stations of the cross.

The young ones with highly technical hair and the rich types caught on quickly enough to the protocols of worship. Everyone was remarkably slow to understand the function of the collection plates. Most seemed to pass them along as if they carried a contagious disease.

The newcomers peppered her with questions at the door on their way out.

"Do you baptize?"

"Yes."

"Can we use your church hall as a jam space?"

"Yes."

"Can I bring my dog?"

"Yes."

"Do you do same-sex marriage?"

"Yes."

"Do you do funerals?"

"Yes."

"Do you do confession?"

"Yes."

"Can I pick your berries?"

"Yes."

"Do I need to wear a shirt?"

"During services, yes."

Then the collection plates began to fill, not always with money, but with packets of marijuana, painted rocks, gift cards to local coffee shops. Then the collection plates began to overflow. Mrs. Dee found deeper ones, more like ornate buckets, to pass around.

Once in a while, a selection of mushrooms presented themselves in the collection. They were always accompanied by a hand-drawn label. Morels, liberty caps, and the pricey matsutake. Christine handed the fungi off to Mrs. Dee, who, after inspecting them, handed them off to the Sisters. Even the potent, reality-altering liberty caps, which produce powerful hallucinations. Where's the harm? The Sisters aren't likely to become addicts. So maybe their contemplations have some zing now and again? The Sisters began to come on Sundays. Larry was back in the fold, and he picked them up in a cargo van. They loved it.

Christine sets down the collection accounts and picks up some unopened mail. A few very official-looking envelopes have piled up from the municipality. The water utility is reporting sharp fluctuations in water use. There is a big yellow exclamation point on the bill. Christine is reminded in curt legal language of the zoning of parish lands. She is reminded also that although growing marijuana is now legal, bypassing utilities is illegal, dangerous, and punishable by heavy fines.

Next, she picks up the opened letter from the bishop that arrived a few weeks back. He is not a fan of email and does everything old-timey. Christine enjoys this and everything else about the bishop. He was brave enough to lay hands on her, for one thing, his steady, strong hands on her head during her ordination. The letter informs her of him coming to visit and to bless the labyrinth. He's coming the day they commemorate Saint Francis of Assisi, which is October 4. She'd better get that window fixed and sort out the labyrinth. Mrs. Dee has posted a "Use at Own Peril" sign at the entrance. Not that it keeps people away. There has been a steady stream of labyrinth users over the summer. Some, in their journey through it, try to stomp down the bricks. It does seem to be having an effect, just like the steps of Montmartre, the ones worn at the very top from pilgrims' knees.

Actually, it's not like that at all. The labyrinth is super ugly, a hazard, and now the bishop wants to come bless it.

Mrs. Dee knocks and comes in from the church entrance.

"Mrs. Stipenheind is here, Reverend, and would like to know if you have a minute."

"Of course."

"Mrs. Stipenheind, right through here. Can I bring the two of you some tea?"

Christine defers to her visitor, who is wearing a cool grey linen suit and who politely declines tea as she pulls up a chair on the other side of Christine's desk.

"What can I do you for you, Mrs. Stipenheind?"

The woman waits until Mrs. Dee has closed the door. Mrs. Stipenheind crosses her legs, sits upright, and looks neither right nor left but straight at Christine.

"My daughter is pregnant."

"Well, congratulations."

"Yes, it's ... Well, it's a miracle." She uncrosses her legs and leans forward, as if she is about to tell a forbidden secret. "You see, they couldn't. Before. Conceive."

"I see."

"Until the wedding." Mrs. Stipenheind pauses, as if trying to decide what to say next.

Christine gives a slight nod and lowers her eyes.

"The groom's family is very concerned about *lineage*." A shadow of what might be distaste crosses her face. "And of course, a video of the ceremony was posted to social media."

Christine raises an eyebrow. "I see."

"Well, I won't bore you with the details, but when the news of their pregnancy was posted, there ... on social media, you know." Mrs. Stipenheind allows an eyebrow to rise. "Well, you see, a comment was made about the water, the water that broke that window. It's gone viral, you see, that it was the water."

"The water."

"It was the water, breaking in like that, they say, that made her fertile. Her womb."

They both look at each other.

"I don't really know what to say."

"Well, don't say anything, Reverend." Tears are coming now. Mrs. Stipenheind quickly dabs them away with a tissue she pulls from her purse. "I'm just very grateful. I've been so worried about my daughter. What she was doing to her body to get pregnant." She shakes her head slightly and rolls her eyes.

"Anyway, I'm a good Anglican. My family were all good Anglicans. My grandparents are buried here."

"Of course. Of course." Christine can tell Mrs. Stipenheind has more to say. The phone rings. Christine waves it off while Mrs. Stipenheind stands up.

"No, I'm finished. Your organ. I'm fixing it. Spare no expense. I know how much these things cost. Have them bill me directly." She leaves her card on Christine's desk and leaves through the door that leads into the church.

The phone is still ringing. Finally, she answers it. It's the RCMP officer who came by at Easter.

"Can you come in today, Reverend?"

She feels the hair on her arms stand on end. She shouldn't be shocked—she knew they would bring her in eventually. "Yes. What time is good?"

"Two o'clock?"

"Okay. Are you at that tiny depot?" Oops. What is she saying?

"That's the one. The *tiny* depot," he says. Is that bitterness she hears in his voice?

"Who will be at the interview, may I ask?"

"Yes, you may ask."

Christine waits. "Is the interview with the RCMP only?"

"Well, I hate to disappoint you."

"I mean to say, will the Military Police be involved in this process?"

"No. That MP was out of place the other day. I informed his office that this missing persons case falls entirely under our jurisdiction."

"I see."

"We always get our man."

"You do."

"See you at two, Reverend."

She should have arranged an earlier time, to get it over with. Her heart is racing. And it's not excitement over the organ. What do they know?

It's almost eleven. Three hours of this till the interview. There is an eleven-thirty aikido at the recreation centre. It's close to the depot and will calm her down. Christine hasn't been to a class in years. She finds her martial arts gear, packs a shower bag, tells Mrs. Dee that she's off, and hops in her car.

SO FAR SO GOOD. Christine is already drenched in sweat eight minutes into the warm-up. She has studied under this teacher for over a decade but has never risen above a white belt. Military life didn't allow for clubs or hobbies.

Besides, her hand-to-hand combat training far exceeds anything being done here. There's no belt for what she knows. The last thing you do is advertise it.

It seems that Sensei Raphael's class has grown. She recognizes a few law enforcement types. There's Richard, a pleasant older man, highly skilled. Sparring with him is enjoyable.

And there is Suzette. Thick Suzette, in the head, but also she's built like a lumberjack. Suzette has a crush on the sensei and doesn't like other women coming near him. Raphael is French, handsome, and charming. Suzette thinks it's cute to hurt Christine when no one is looking. She hopes Raphael has this sorted out because you can't really have that at a recreation centre. A big, dumb, baboon bully injuring all the females in a martial arts class.

On her piece of the mat, Christine is rolling back and forth. They are supposed to be doing a hundred rolls. Today it'll be more like twenty. Christine tucks her neck, meets the floor, rolls along the bony top edge of her shoulders, and stands back up. More like hurls herself upright. Roll eight complete. She checks the clock. Only one minute has passed since the last time she looked.

Warm-up isn't really the right word for what they are doing. It is a high-intensity, full-body workout that warns the body of the kind of impact that is coming in the second half of the class.

After the warm-up, they sit quietly while the sensei goes over technique. Christine shifts from sitting on her heels to sitting cross-legged. Cramps are beginning to assert themselves. She has spent the better part of the last three years sitting. She sits there almost panting, and so hot she feels like the skin might peel off her face.

The sensei makes a joke about this. "Oh ho ho ho! You are old and fat away from the mat."

Even with her legs folded underneath her, the cramps in her calves return. She needs to stand up. How much longer is he going to take to teach this basic action? Even though the uniform is made of cotton, it's too tightly woven. It doesn't breathe. She can feel hot air rushing up from her core past her face. She can tell her face is red.

Suzette has always been allowed to wear spandex. Today it is gunmetal grey, with shiny, raised black lines that serve no performance purpose whatsoever.

They break into sparring partners. As Christine stands up, she feels blood rush back into her legs. She finds Richard and makes her way toward him where he's standing on the firm, well-used tatami mat. He sees her too and is moving toward her when Suzette moves in between them with as much grace as a wrecking ball. Christine notices that some brave soul has attempted to break up her monobrow.

"Hi there, killer," Suzette greets her.

"Hi, Suzette." To Christine's dismay, Richard partners up with one of the law enforcement types. Everyone else has already paired up, and she's stuck with Suzette.

Sure enough, Suzette gets a death grip on her arm and wrenches it back, in a direction her shoulder just doesn't want to go, as she tosses Christine onto the mat.

Christine has always cut Suzette slack. Suzette has anger issues. Suzette has no self-confidence. Suzette is working through bully issues from childhood. But mostly, Suzette is a civilian. The charges for hurting them are serious. July thirtieth, Christine. Not January. Just a little longer—tomorrow.

Christine tells herself that she is powerless over Suzette. God will sort out Suzette. Christine is not the police of the world. Love thy neighbour, love thine enemy, just love. Love, love, love. Love is giving and wise.

Christine attempts to roll her shoulder back into the vicinity of where it should be and rubs it. Suzette comes at Christine again. With the elegance and circular movement aikido is known for, Christine throws Suzette. Suzette lands right where Christine intends for her to land, past the edge of the mat, on the hardwood floor.

Bony contact points of Suzette's limbs connect with the gym's wood floor. Bare skin squeaks and burns on the polished surface. The centripetal force of aikido is like a hurricane, and provides a nice velocity when you know what you're doing. The shiny, raised black lines of Suzette's spandex squeak a little too. They are a nice touch after all.

All ten pairs stop sparring, look over, and move to form a circle around Suzette on the floor. With a toss of his perfectly coiffed dark hair, Raphael takes a knee beside her.

"Suzette, oh *pauvre* Suzette. Is anything broken? Take your time—let me know when to help you up."

The flat-faced cop says, "That's assault."

Christine furrows her brow. "We were sparring too close to the edge—it was an accident." Christine looks at the sanctimonious cop. "I feel so bad."

Raphael keeps muttering that he will make it all right. What a hero. Suzette smiles meltingly. Raphael somehow manages to hoist Suzette onto a chair. Then, rubbing his chest, he lowers his head and walks onto the tatami mats. Once in the middle of the mat, he raises his head high. His eyes have darkened with seriousness. He thrusts both hands out and lowers them. They are to sit and watch.

With the invitational aikido curtsy, Raphael, a black belt in multiple martial arts, stretches out a hand toward Christine. They will now spar.

"Somebody needs more instruction, yes?"

The class grows silent. They know they are in for a show. The silence is broken by the slam of Christine's body hitting the tatami mat once, twice, three times. By the seventh time, Christine notices something. It is almost as if a little shard of the dark, hard rock in her heart breaks off on impact. It feels good. She wants as many pieces possible knocked clear out of her.

After the fifteenth time, it becomes clear that her heart will not be cleansed of the horrors of her past. Raphael is now getting rough. He must be tired. Some of her prior injuries begin to inform her that she is too old for this. A wrist that broke thirty years ago, a disk in her spine that exploded during a jump, with fragments now lodged in her sciatic nerve. She is no longer landing well. She stands up, adjusts her uniform, and rejects his beckoning.

"Enough."

"Oh no, ho ho ho, *mon cherie*, it is I that tell you when it is enough." Raphael comes at her. Christine moves with him, absorbing the power of his attack, takes his wrist, and whirls him around her centre in a spin. All hear the sweep of Raphael's feet leaving the mat as she glides him up high for the takedown. Once down, she relocates his wrist and elbow for an arm bar turn on his face, completely incapacitating him. She hears an impressed grunt behind her from one of the onlookers.

With a final twist of his arm, Christine calmly says "No," moves away from him, and in a moment is picking up her shower bag by the door. She opens the door with her hips, looks back into the room, and sees the cop helping Raphael up. Sensei's eyes flash at her.

"Don't come back here."

It is now 1:50 and Christine is parked outside the RCMP depot with the car still running. The drive wasn't long enough for the air conditioning to cool the vehicle. Christine is still sweating and in her aikido uniform. She pulls down the mirror. She has puffy patches under her eyes, which look glazed.

Christine has the air conditioning knob all the way to the right. She opens her bag and pulls out her clothing. Pants are easy, except that she is still so sweaty that they cling. She nearly rips them pulling them on.

Christine reclines her driver's seat all the way and takes off the belted kimono top. Whew. Lost her deodorant on the mat, apparently. Christine takes off her sports bra next. Suzette did some more damage to her shoulder. Predators, even stupid ones, always sniff out weakness. She should have just left the bra on because now her shoulder is completely seized. She can barely move it.

Christine focuses on the cool air blowing over her, drying her sweat. She reaches into her bag for her crystal deodorant. She dropped it in her hotel room in Ottawa and it shattered. She fishes out a sizable piece. It needs to be moistened with water to apply it. Not a drop of water in her car. She uses this crystal one because it is supposed to be safe for women. No aluminum chlorohydrate, it states on the lid, beside a pink ribbon.

Christine licks the piece in her hand. Not bad. Tangy, like juice crystals. She licks it a few times and is about to apply it when a manicured hand with long purple nails taps on her driver's side window. Christine whips her good arm over her bare breasts. A woman wearing an RCMP jacket and aviators brings her talon-like hand up to her mouth to suck on a cigarette. There are jewels in the nails that glint in the sun.

When she exhales, she also points to a sign and reads to Christine: "No Idling Zone." Christine shuts off her car and hopes this will send the woman away. She waits patiently for talon fingers to at least stop staring. She doesn't. Christine has obviously parked where this woman takes a cigarette break, and nothing is going to interfere with her nicotine fix.

Christine tries to keep her face as nonconfrontational as possible and waits for her to leave. At 1:57 p.m., the smoke break is complete.

Christine struggles to put on her regular bra. It's not going to happen. She forgoes the bra and painfully puts on a crisp, collared shirt and a blazer.

Christine flips the mirror down again to inspect. Her hair is all over the place. She looks at her hands. She is about to spit-style her hair. Her hands smell of Suzette's perfume and Raphael's nasty cologne. She doesn't want to spread that around. She pulls out a dry shampoo sample she got somewhere.

It sprays out a forceful mist. It crusts onto her dark roots and her blazer. Christine combs it through her hair. Now she looks like a fifties greaser with dandruff.

At the door, she yanks on the metal door handle, the cloud of sweet smell around her vaguely familiar. Why the fuck doesn't the door open? The intercom sparks and crackles as the resigned, fed-up voice of the smoker hits her ears. "Please read the sign that is posted in both official languages and follow instructions." She's on camera. She needs all her self-control to stop from rolling her eyes.

She reads the sign that has been laminated with many pieces

of packing tape. She presses the intercom button. "Hello, this Christine Wright. I have an appointment at two o'clock with Constable ..." What is his last name? She doesn't even know. This is so rude.

"Cleveland."

"Right. Constable Cleveland."

At 2:02, Christine walks into the lobby. She's late. For a police interview. Bad form. The constable is waiting for her with a big file in his hand.

"Jackie tells me you two met outside." Jackie, now behind safety glass without the aviators, shares a look with the constable.

"Right. No idling. Sorry about that."

"We wondered if you missed us. You know, we're so tiny." He pauses, hiding a smile. "Now that you're finally here, let's get started. Follow me this way."

Christine follows the constable into a reinforced concrete-walled interview room that will be here after an earthquake of any magnitude. Recording equipment is embedded in the wall opposite the two-way mirror.

As she pulls her chair out, she suddenly places the smell of the dry shampoo. Like candy floss on top of butane, sickly sweet notes mingle with the underlay of harsh chemicals. Christine gently lowers her aching body onto the thinly padded chair, her clothes hum with the telltale perfume of someone who has just smoked crystal meth.

The constable sits down and looks Christine directly in the eye. He has not yet switched on the recording equipment. The camera's light is off. He precisely adjusts his chair and sits back in it, perfectly at ease with himself. Christine, on the other hand, has begun to sweat again. It's a hot summer day and the damn room is hot.

It won't be long before she sweats through these pants. Her chair doesn't adjust. The mustard-coloured seat cover isn't dark enough. She will leave a sweaty ass mark on the cloth. Christine looks down. Has she at least done up her fly? Yes. Well, that's something at least. The constable still isn't saying a word. Maybe he is waiting for her to speak first.

"This depot, it's interesting, eh? All these different—what would you call them?—uh, levels of governance intersecting. Most people don't even know there is an RCMP presence here."

Nothing. He doesn't say anything.

"I don't mean to say—"

"That's one way to look at it. The way it's all been sliced up. Interesting. That's a word for it." Then he switches on the recording device and begins the interview preamble. He states her name, his name, the date, all the usual, including that Terrence Devonshire, the missing person in question, is now presumed dead. The red light on the camera turns on.

The air conditioning kicks in. It's so loud that he raises his voice. "I've asked to talk to you about the events of Friday, April 17 …" Christine finds herself staring at the guy's knuckles. They look soft, like they've never punched anyone. This is disappointing.

"Christine?" She looks up.

He continues. "We have an eyewitness who states they saw Terrence Devonshire enter the office of your church at approximately 8:45. Yet the information you gave his common-law spouse, Shawna Devonshire, is in conflict with this eyewitness report."

Christine knows enough to wait for a direct question and says nothing.

"Can you please take me through the events as clearly as possible?"

Christine resists the urge to shift in her seat. Shifting might fend off an ass mark but will make her look nervous. Droplets are trickling down her back.

"Yes. That is correct. Terry did enter the church office. I felt it was preferable to maintain discretion about this when speaking with Shawna. Terry was, in fact, welcomed and entered the office for the rite of confession. We began, and he then had a change of heart and left suddenly. I didn't want to upset his spouse further nor break the sanctity of the confession, so I did not inform Shawna of his visit when she asked me."

The constable has one paper form on the desk beside the bulging file that remains closed. Christine gathers, by a little discreet upside-down reading, that this is a presumption of death statement. She believes this has to go to a judge to be validated.

"Do you have any other information regarding the whereabouts of Terrence Devonshire?"

"I wish I could help." She's obviating a direct yes or no answer and wonders if he'll take it. She has stopped sweating. The room is now cool. Icy. In the lengthy pause that ensues, Christine's nipples begin to voice their concern over how much longer this is going to take. Christine curves her chest inwards to keep them away from the shirt that was starched by Mrs. Dee.

She remembers her discharge interview from the psych unit after her suicide attempt. She decided to wear an ultracomfortable microfibre bralette and she could feel that her left breast had slipped underneath the flimsy thing at the beginning of the interview. This rogue breast was all she could think about as the doctor asked: "Do you have any unwanted thoughts? Any disturbing images interrupting or intruding?" No. Only this left breast that's trying to make me look crazy. A wild, crazy woman who cannot control her breasts.

"And what time was this?" the constable asks.

"Sometime around nine o'clock."

"And he was alone?"

"Yes, he was alone."

The constable concludes the interview and shuts off the recording equipment. His movements are slow and deliberate. Now he opens the large file.

The air conditioner is blasting and she is shivering. The air is thin. She isn't breathing properly. There is a tunnel encroaching on the outskirts of her vision. Raphael hadn't landed her with a lot of skill. While she had been playing rag doll, Christine had hit her head a few times.

She tries to sit up straight, to roll her shoulders back. The nipples don't like this at all. She watches the constable lay out nine photos and turn them so they are face up for Christine. Seven are of women. One is a newspaper clipping of an elderly man and a burnt-out building. Six of the images of the females have the eyes barred to protect their privacy while capturing various injuries. Terry likes to break noses and knock out teeth. The seventh is a school photo of a teenage girl. Christine recognizes her as a young overdose victim from a documentary on the opioid crisis and child prostitution.

The constable's jaw is set. "Do you know what you are looking at?"

Before she can speak, he says, "This is Terry's file."

It becomes clear that Christine is not supposed to speak.

"Jackie and I have had our eye on him for quite some time."

Christine can see the constable's breath. She can see the fog of her own breath mingle with his above the photos laid out on the table. All those lives destroyed, lives ended. The older gentleman was killed in that hotel fire five years back. The newspaper clipping is a piece on organized crime slumlords cashing in on insurance. He looks like a grandfather.

The tunnel is narrowing, and she can hardly see the photos, the tabletop. She forces air in and out of her lungs.

"We are presuming Terry is dead. I hope he is. I don't want this file added to. I'd like to shake the hand of the person who punched this guy's ticket."

Christine places a hand on the desk for her forehead to land on and tucks her chin slightly so she won't smash her face, but now the constable is standing, he's opening the door. Christine forces herself to stand.

Warm air spills into the ice locker. She is moving. Sharp electrical twinges fire through her legs and hips as she puts one foot ahead of the other. The constable stops her at the door to shake her hand. Cool air is blowing past her legs and flooding into the foyer.

Christine forces a nod from her stiff neck as she passes Jackie.

Somehow she's outside the depot, blinking in the sun. The intercom crackles behind her. Bloody hell, now what?

"Uh, Reverend, it's Jackie. I run a choir, and I heard your place has great acoustics."

Christine stops and turns her rigid body just enough so that her voice will reach the speaker. "Yes, please come by, any time."

Now she must keep going to the car. Once inside, she carefully places the seat belt over her painfully thawing nipples. She waits until she is blocks away before she starts telling her breasts that everything is going to be okay.

MRS. DEE WAITS patiently for the Reverend to arrive. She is beyond late and has almost completely missed their Summer's End Market Fair. Everyone else has made an effort. Even the weather has co-operated. It's a hot, clear day with no wind. The only trouble is all this vermin. The crows and squirrels are being pesky. The fairgoers have been harassed all day by the mice, the rats, the chipmunks, and whatever else was attracted by all that birdseed scattered across the labyrinth.

It has brought Mrs. Dee enormous pleasure, watching the Reverend throwing that seed about day after day. She indeed got quite a laugh out of her switch job. Birdseed for ecograss. After a few weeks, the Reverend asked Mrs. Dee about the grass. When would it sprout? The seed disappeared, and yet no grass sprouted.

"You'll see, Reverend. There will be a lush green rug for the bishop to walk over. For the price we paid, it's almost guaranteed."

It was delightful when all the little creatures began to arrive. But now Mrs. Dee is having some misgivings. She has seen a coyote lingering behind the game fence. Where there's one coyote, there are more.

If she hadn't been blinded by rage, she could have done something with roses or even planted some almond trees at that price. What a waste. Well, not for the mice and whatnot. They of course are feasting on it daily. She wonders what she can do about the situation now that things have gone this far.

It is a hot day. She has had to keep her eye on Mrs. Wilson and

Mr. Fowler. People need reminding to keep up their hydration in the heat. Everyone can do without a case of heatstroke.

It was decided that the Summer's End Market was to take place in the parking lot this year. The front entrances of the church and hall are perpendicular to each other, each on the edge of the main parking lot. Having the fair here is a first, and it is due to the fact that the labyrinth is just such a mess. Bricks are still coming loose. People might trip. And of course, as Mrs. Wilson said, "Rats are just not an attraction, are they?"

Both she and Mrs. Wilson had toiled in the hot sun for this event. Evan had come to help with the tables. He teamed up with Mrs. Wilson, and together they had persuaded her to put some of her drawings on display.

One of the hippy types quickly sold out of their gluten-free hashish brownies. The Buddhists also have a few tables set up, some draped with colourful prayer flags. Now she is listening to a Buddhist educate Larry.

The tanned girl with curly hair tells Larry, "The Buddha taught what Jesus brought. I think of Jesus as a bodhisattva."

"What's that?" Larry asks. "A kind of buddha?"

"Sort of. Someone who is fully capable of reaching nirvana but purposefully delays doing so out of compassion to save those who suffer."

"Hmm. Wow." They both grow quiet.

There are harvest tables from local farms, some pottery, second-hand china and jewellery. The Sisters brought their preserves and are sporting grey, full-face sun visors, a gift from some South Korean Sisters during the pandemic. The good Sisters look like characters from an Atwood novel.

A witchy-looking woman who has been coming to services lately flits about all the tables. With white hair down to her hips, she struts around in her yellow skirt and sandals. Moving like every step is a victory, her head held high, her back is so arched that Mrs. Dee sees her as a banana. A banana with an insistently talkative mouth.

Of course, this talking banana isn't here to purchase anything. She just pulls up a chair beside the person she has taken hostage and talks at them. Her goal is immediate intimacy with each of her victims. How undignified. Her animated body language alone makes Mrs. Dee tired. Why don't people act their age?

The witch turns toward Mrs. Dee's table. Mrs. Dee holds her breath. She glances at Mrs. Wilson, who is sitting next to her. With a sigh of relief, she watches surreptitiously as the banana makes her way over to Mrs. Wilson. Without asking, she pulls away a chair from another table, places it too close to Mrs. Wilson's left, and sits down.

"Have you always been a Christian, Mrs. Wilson?"

Mrs. Wilson quickly moves even closer to the hostage taker. "You could say I was born one."

"No one is born a Christian," the witch snorts.

Mrs. Wilson waves away her hand dismissively. "Why, just after they smacked my ass in the delivery room I was baptized, yes I was."

"Is that so?"

"Can't give the Devil a chance, can we?"

A slick, black Mercedes with tinted back windows pulls into the main parking lot in front of the hall and church. It screams of prestige and commands the eye as it quickly manoeuvres a dough-nut and comes to a silent stop on the edge of the market. After a pause, the driver emerges. He looks like an Olympic athlete. His suit is merely a thin layer over top bulging muscles. All the Sisters' space-age visors are facing his way. Who on earth is that?

He opens the rear passenger door and a very chic woman emerges. Mrs. Wilson murmurs, "That's the maid of honour, from the Stipenheind-Bluefield wedding." All the summer fairgoers are transfixed as the stunning woman floats by in head-to-toe designer clothing. A long, salmon-coloured, woven blazer over a white, button-up blouse and impeccably tailored grey pants. The blouse looks like silk. When the fabric is of that quality, one can still dress in the heat.

"Not really a maid, is she?" Larry asks. Sunglasses and scarf strategically protect her from any prying eyes. The witchy one abandons her chair by Mrs. Wilson and trots over to this glamorous woman like a curious dog.

The glamorous woman's posture is wide and open as she languidly greets the curious little dog. No one can hear what they say to each other as they make their way to the labyrinth. Once near the middle, the witch points to the centre of the labyrinth and then points over to the broken missionary window about thirty feet away. She begins to re-enact the gushing of the labyrinth water by holding her hands together over her head, as if to leap and launch herself through the window.

The woman opens her purse, pulls something out, and quickly stoops down at the centre of the labyrinth. Actually, it's more of a swoop. A woman like that doesn't stoop.

"What?" Mrs. Dee catches herself saying out loud.

Bill, the honey vendor, pipes up, "Looks as though she's collected some mud from the labyrinth."

Bill, Larry, and Mrs. Dee all stare as the witchy woman performs some undulating dance moves while rubbing her vulva.

"Oh my God," Mrs. Dee says.

"What?" Mr. Fowler intercedes. "Sometimes we need to scratch." Mrs. Dee wishes no longer to witness this. She looks instead at

Mr. Fowler, who is dressed in one of those skirts for men and is standing stock-still in front of her table.

He notices her noticing. "I must say," he whispers, "it's the wretched clothing that makes us so uncomfortable. This attire obviates any need for shifting. All is—how shall I say this?—free."

Beside him is a young man with no shirt, wearing a similar sarong and sandals. He is holding a very large hallucinogenic mushroom in his hands like a young child holds a candle during Santa Lucia. The mushroom's shiny, sloped peak is missing a tiny nibble. *Psilocybe azurescens* or Blue Coyote is her guess. Very potent. His lip is blue. He better fasten his seat belt, he's in for quite a ride.

The young man has not properly bathed in some time, and because he's rather short and stout and grubby, with earth on his hands, he looks like a forest gnome. She checks Mr. Fowler's lips for blue and is relieved to see none. At least Mr. Fowler is wearing a shirt.

"Come on, let's get some kombucha," Mr. Fowler says to his forest gnome friend. "Mrs. Dee?"

"No, thank you, Mr. Fowler. It's a bit too rambunctious for my palate."

Mr. Fowler looks over his sunglasses at her. "Are you so very sure about that, Mrs. Dee?"

Mrs. Dee sees that the maid of honour is getting into her car. The driver, in one elegant movement, takes the vial of mud, opens the door, and steps in between his passenger and the witchy personage, her new companion.

"Quite. Yes, quite sure, Mr. Fowler. No kombucha for me today. Thanks all the same."

The parading banana makes her way straight over to Mrs. Dee. It is finally her turn to entertain the witch, it seems.

"So, what is the queen's role in this denomination?"

Bloody hell.

"I see little crowns everywhere. What's the deal? I just took my citizenship test, so I studied this stuff, but I still don't get it. The deal with the queen, you know."

This stuff. Mrs. Dee tries to take a slow easy breath. "King Henry placed himself as the head of the Church."

The witchy one likes that. "Instead of the Pope."

"Yes, that's right. Instead of the Pope."

The witchy one offers, "Sort of like when the druids got rid of the Romans."

"Well, I hadn't thought of it like that. Did the druids get rid of the Romans?"

"Was that before or after he executed his wives?" The witch asks.

"Let's see, I think"—

"So he began the English Reformation."

Mrs. Dee tries to conclude. "Yes, and Elizabeth the First implemented it, correcting a severe power imbalance."

"I don't think so," the witch snorts.

"What do you mean?"

"Wasn't she the one who sent those morons over here to take whatever they wanted?" The witch's movements lose any sense of her banana whimsy and she is suddenly taut, almost rigid.

"Yes, well, I see what you mean," Mrs. Dee mutters.

"I mean *whatever* they wanted." She turns her head toward the graves. "Are there any unmarked Indigenous graves here?"

Mrs. Dee gasps. "What a question!"

"Typical response for someone who's in it." The witch makes a circle with a pointed finger.

"In what, exactly?" Mrs. Dee raises her eyebrows.

"You're caught up completely in the colonizing machine."

The witch looks over at the window. "That window. The one that broke? Disgusting. Why on earth would something like that be enshrined?"

They both look at the cardboard and duct tape on the missionary window in question.

"Ms …"

"Call me Ananda."

"Ananda, I'll have you know that I am in full control of my faculties and I for one am greatly relieved that window is broken."

This Ananda, in a most irritating fashion, does have a point. Canadians overdo the crown business. The crown this, the crown that. Maybe the crown should grow some royal balls as St. Paul might say and own some of the devastation wrought on so many peoples.

The Reverend appears from the residence's parking lot. She's all smiles as she hobbles toward them. She winces with each step, and she has one arm clutched to her chest.

"Are you all right?"

"I will be after a hot bath."

"A hot bath? In this heat?"

The witchy woman was not going to pass this up. Moving her open hand around in a circular motion as if scanning Christine with it, she intones, "I am deducing that you've stopped wearing a bra? You know, Reverend, there are exercises that help strengthen the breast tissue." She arches her back and begins to massage her breasts through her tight tank top. "You cannot quit bras cold turkey." She is playing with her nipples now. "After some time, the power of the body is unleashed."

Mrs. Dee averts her eyes. How grotesque.

"Is that so? Mrs. Dee, are these yours?" Christine's eyes are not on the witch's nipples, they are on the drawings. The Reverend, thank God for small mercies, will not be discussing her breasts or feeling them up at the Summer's End Fair.

"Yes. I joined the drawing group."

"Oh, art is so vital in this world." The witch begins a lengthy discourse on her thoughts on this topic. Art is truth. Art subverts all power. Art breaks chains. Blah blah blah. What a windbag.

Mrs. Wilson quickly jumps up from her seat and begins to leaf through the drawings. She pulls one out of the pile and places it on the easel. Everyone falls silent.

Except the witch. "This drawing is astonishing. Do you not feel a deep, rushing peace filling the mind? Silence stealing softly over your heart?"

"Yes, it's beautiful. Is that Mary?" the Reverend asks. Good grief, the Reverend's eyes have filled and her chin is trembling.

"No, that's Susan, one of our life models. There, there now, maybe you should go have that bath." This is not exactly what the Summer's End Market Fair needs, a braless Reverend who appears now to be copiously weeping.

"I know, I *know* what this is!" The witch will not be silenced and grasps the Reverend's hand as Christine tries to limp away. "It's the window. The new window! To replace the broken one." She is gesticulating wildly, like a windmill. "She is aware of the past but there is newness in her eyes, moving toward an event. A great event!"

The Reverend is now headed for her residence, walking like a broken doll. She calls back over her shoulder, "Great idea. Let's get it done before the bishop comes, Mrs. Dee."

Mrs. Dee sits dumbfounded as the witch wanders from table to table informing the whole Summer's End Fair of the upcoming new window. The Sisters all cluck in approval. Now everyone is talking about the possibilities of the window. It will bring in a new era. It will be a symbol of reconciliation. This window is now about to solve the world's problems. That's right. No pressure.

While placing her drawings and easel in her Prius, Mrs. Dee grows hotter than the afternoon sun beating down on them. Let's get it done? How dare the Reverend! How dare they! Power imbalance indeed! What about the workhorses of the church, just whip them until they are dead?

Lowering herself into her seat, she feels tightness all through her solar plexus right down into her pelvic floor. She is not like that witchy woman. Her back doesn't arch the way hers does, it does the opposite. Her body curves over her heart, to protect it. Buckling her seatbelt, she finds she's on the verge of tears. Her heart is unprotected and open for a moment until she quickly crosses it with the belt. She is short on breath. This is too much pressure to put on anyone. They ask too much.

CHRISTINE HAS NOW been soaking in the deep bathtub for a few hours, and she can feel the four hundred milligrams of ibuprofen easing her battered muscles. She keeps reheating as much as the hot water tank will allow. The bathwater is reminiscent of the Dead Sea with the amount of Epsom salts she has added. The aching has stopped. She feels almost whole. She is not getting out of this bath for anyone.

Her phone chirps. It's Joey.

"Need a favour."

This is rare. More than rare. This is a never.

"Name it."

"I need a plus-one-and-reference."

"Okay. When?"

"Now."

Christine puts her phone down on the chair beside the tub and stands up. It's not pretty. Her flesh is puffy and wrinkled from several hours in the tub and there is a dark purple bruise on her hip. She steps out of the tub, slips, and grabs onto the towel rack. It rips clean off the wall.

"I need you in a collar."

She puts the rack on the floor. "Why?"

"Interview with Benedictines."

Joey's considering entering into community. He wants to retire into one. The Benedictines' doors had closed during the pandemic. They must be taking people in again. The idea of not having Joey around is too much for her to think about right now.

"The Scot's Caber. Five."

What a strange place for an interview—the pub where Christine nearly threw herself back into the booze. It has a great kitchen, not just a lot of single malt and beer. Christine hopes Joey has managed reservations or they'll be waiting for hours.

Christine selects her most modern clergy blouse. It's made of a fluid matte satin and cut to drape beautifully. The sleeves allow a little of her tattoo to peak through at the wrist. As she zips up her high-waisted, wide-legged pants, she winces. Her ribs are not at all properly aligned. She can feel at least one rib has torqued into her lung. She cannot breathe in fully without feeling a sharp poke. Well, her ribs and the towel rack will have to wait. It's go time. It's show-up-for-Joey time.

TOM COUNTS THIS as the fourth time that Shawna has flirted with the waiter. This place used to be a church. Now it's a gastropub. Some of the waiters wear kilts.

"How do you know so much about wine?" she says with a slur. Shawna giggles and bats her eyelashes over her huge doll eyes. There are so many coats of mascara on her eyelashes, they look like tarantulas.

"Is this a test or a tease?" The waiter is flirting back with her now. He's Scottish. That accent must be panty remover.

Tom finds himself feeling jealous. What's up with that? Pay no mind. Should be thanking this Scottish dude. Go ahead, take her off my hands, please.

Once Shawna has selected her second bottle of wine, the waiter leaves. The candlelight is not flattering. Shawna set the makeup gun to max tonight. The heavy black stuff around her eyes makes the dark circles stand out.

"Thank you so much for coming to my celebration, Tom."

"Hey. Thanks for the invite. I don't eat out. So expensive, you know? You sure? I can pay."

Shawna tosses her waist-length hair over one shoulder. "No, I said I would pay. Anyway, what do you do anyway?"

"I'm in autobody. Mostly collision repair. But I—"

"Right. I think I knew that. Sorry. Yeah, not the most lucrative. Autobody. Did I tell you I'm back at work? I'm an emergency nurse. They're rehiring anyone with qualifications. I just got on at the General."

"Is that what we're celebrating? Your new job?"

Shawna puts both hands around her wineglass and flips her hair over to the other shoulder. Then she leans over the table toward him and hovers over the tea light candle. This girl is whacked. She looks like a rat. A long-haired rat.

"Ouch! That's hot!" She blows out the candle and leans in closer. Tom can smell the mix of cigarettes and white wine on her breath.

"No, that's not what I'm celebrating. They had to take me back. They're desperate."

"Um."

"I fucking hate working at the hospital. I had to go back. I had no money."

"Oh."

"No, it's about what my Military Police friend has managed to do."

"Mmm."

Shawna looks annoyed. "You know, Tom, words would be good. You just make sounds with people. Are you even interested? Do you even make words? You're not in the autobody shop here."

Tom decides not to tell Ron about this dinner.

"You didn't even find out anything about Terry. Like, don't you care?" No, Ron will just restate how girls like Shawna are his drug of choice. That he needs to clear up his codependency issues.

"Don't you care what I'm going through? What me and my child are going through?"

Ron will remind Tom that he can't fix his insides by fixing his outsides. He needs to stop saving others. Save himself.

His guts are churning. He doesn't want to be here with her, but here he is. He knows better. Getting involved with Shawna could throw his whole future into jeopardy. He's about to become an addictions counsellor. Just finished a practicum after years of night school. Just waiting for the credential.

"Yes, I care, Shawna. Tell me."

"Okay. Well, it's good. That Military Police guy knows Christine is involved and is going to get the RCMP to interview her."

"How does this MP know?"

"He says that he knows her from before and that she's a real piece of shit."

The waiter interrupts with the second bottle. "My, you are a thirsty lass this evening."

"Insatiable!" Shawna is already too loud. "Ha. Just kidding. We are celebrating. Well, I'm celebrating, and my friend is joining me. Not my boyfriend. Just friend. I'm single."

"Well, that just sounds so festive." The waiter busies himself with the ritual of opening a bottle of wine. She senses his indifference and tries to change his mind. She moves the glass in circles on the table, while flashing those green eyes up at the waiter. A siren waiting on the ocean floor.

The waiter is patient and waits for his chance to fill the glass. He notices the extinguished candle. He strikes a match and lights it. "Let's shed some light on this celebration."

Tom sits back in his chair, relieved. What a messed-up thing to be celebrating. Shawna all but gulps down her entire goblet of wine. When is Shawna going to get cut off? It's not the kind of place where people routinely get blind drunk.

"Apparently, Christine is Military, so that's why he gets to be involved in the investigation."

Shawna is overflowing with joy. Her hair bounces and shimmers.

"What investigation? Terry took off, Shawna. He left."

"No, he didn't. He wouldn't do that. There's something going on. I know she knows. So does the MP."

"Knows what? What are you going on about? There's been a crime? Evidence, Shawna. They need evidence."

"I fucking know that, Tom. He'll get it. He's a cop. Or sort of. He used to be. Anyway, he still has detective skills. Those don't go away. He's going to find out." Shawna downs another entire glass and moans like she is having an orgasm. "Terry can't just fucking walk out on me. No one can. And not with her." She pours herself another glass until it overflows. It's the end of the bottle. "The MP is going to get the RCMP involved, the military, and the legal system."

"What?"

Shawna looks at Tom like he is an idiot. "Are you fucking deaf?" People look over. Shawna's jawline hardens and her whole torso sways. She's wasted. "She's fucking hiding Terry. I know it. She can't do that. He's mine."

Tom can feel himself scowling. She's grossing him out. Why is he here? He can leave any time. He thinks about Terrine and flinches inwardly. Little Terrine can't leave. The beginning chapters of her life have already been a nightmare.

The waiter is back, carrying a large tray heaped with their food. So much food. They're on the upper level, where the choir used to sing. Shawna ordered four vegan appetizers after she had complained of no vegan entrées. After the server set the four dishes down, the reason why he's enduring Shawna is placed in front of him. A sizzling, done-to-perfection, eight-ounce steak with potatoes. After child support, all his money goes to night school. He eats cheap crap out of cans and boxes.

Suddenly, he has no appetite. His meal is being paid for with money that is for Terrine.

Ron's raspy voice tells him to eat up, that he'll need all his strength to play God in this child's life. Tom cuts into the steak. He's not playing God, he's doing the next right thing. That's what he is supposed to do in recovery, isn't it? Do the next right thing?

That's what Ron tells him. Almost every day. Tom's made up his mind. He knows what the next right thing is.

Tom keeps his head down. He's going to ignore Ron's badgering. He's going to ignore the dirty look Shawna is giving the meat eater.

Tom ignores both of them the best he can. He does need his strength. He can't sit back and do nothing here. He was Terry's sponsor. Terry's child is alone with this cruel head case. He knows he can't change Shawna, but that doesn't mean he's going to abandon Terrine.

He forces the food down his throat. Shawna is feasting on her many seared vegetables. He keeps telling himself that as long as that candle burns, he is safe on his side of the table.

CHRISTINE IS DOING her best to fit in and to be smooth at The Scot's Caber. She tries not to scour the streets for threats as she enters. She tries not to analyze the oak-clad interior and the wait staff tactically. Civilians get nervous when she does that. None of that. Smooth, smooth is what we want.

Once she's seated with Joey and his weird friends, she forces her eyes to stay on the menu and her mouth into a neutral line. Smooth.

Why this jam-packed place, with its live music? It doesn't matter. This is for Joey. Christine is there to make sure that Joey shines. This isn't hard to do, because Joey is Joey. Joey always shines.

The two Benedictines are both dressed the part, in long woollen robes with thin leather cinctures. Prayer beads on display, tied to the leather. The Sister is wearing a black veil with white trim farther back on her head, showing some hair. The Brother can talk. He has a lot to say, and he inhales quickly and exhales almost imperceptibly to make sure he can't be interrupted. The Sister makes little sounds with matching faces to indicate that everything the Brother says has great meaning.

"Brother Joey, or do you prefer Joe?" The rosy-cheeked Brother only stops talking long enough to pop another scallop in his mouth and swill down a gulp of ale.

Joey shrugs nonchalantly. "Sure, that works Brother Mike, I like it. Has a good ring to it."

"I can speak for both of us when I say that we're honoured you're considering joining us."

The Sister isn't stuffing her face. She is sitting on her hands, nodding vigorously and rocking back and forth in her chair. She offers, "The work you did with human trafficking, Brother Joe— amazing."

Joey smiles at her. "Not too many people know about that, Sister Josephine."

Christine recognizes that smile from years ago. Spiritual direction with Joey was so special, so intimate, so healing. She can tell Joey anything. The first time they spoke, he smiled and she felt like she had always known him. Joey doesn't smile at her like that anymore. Something in her lower core lurches. A deep muscle near her navel is trying to hang onto Joey. Her shoulder once again is screaming.

Brother Mike keeps going. "So, we really ride that edge between neo-monasticism, radical orthopraxy, and postmodern asceticism."

Christine fights an eye roll. These are not Benedictines. Benedictines don't behave like this. These are just run-of-the-mill do-gooders playing dress-up. One of whom appears to have not eaten in twenty years.

Why did Joey ask her to wear a collar? He's not wearing one. He never does. She doesn't want to be associated with these people. These are people who have given up on their shitty lives to join a cult.

Joey is nodding. Holy shit, Joey is lapping this up. "That's a great place to be today. God in relationship, right? The discipline allows us to wrap ourselves around holy relationship." He's being placed up high on a pedestal and is enjoying the view. Christine's stomach begins to churn.

Brother Mike wraps his mouth around the last scallop. Watch it, Christine. Be smooth. Christine wipes any sneer from her face. She misses the pandemic masks, the gift of sneering in complete privacy.

Everyone but Christine is enjoying themself. The three of them are having a good discussion anyway. The table is cluttered with many plates and beverages. The food has been superb. Many would describe this scene as boisterous, joyous, or convivial. But not her.

Christine has eaten too much. She had to do something while everyone else was yakking away. She regrets this as she struggles to breathe. Right at the end of the inhale, she feels the rib poking where it shouldn't. Her ribs will need adjusting. Her chiropractor has done this for her in the past. Christine excuses herself and heads to the ladies' room.

To her dismay, Sister Josephine rises quickly and follows her. Christine cannot stand female bonding in any form, but especially in the bathroom.

The Sister emerges from her stall in time to wash her hands while Christine is washing hers. "I can see those marks," Sister Josephine murmurs. Her eyes are on Christine's arms, exposed while her sleeves are bunched up above her wrists. Is mark a medieval term for tattoo? "Have you thought about taking the Rule of Saint Benedict, Mother?"

Christine looks at the Sister's reflection in the mirror. Fifteen years of military service has given Christine more discipline in her pinky finger than Saint Benedict had in his entire body.

"That does not seem to be my path, Sister." Christine checks her face in the mirror for the smooth kindness she wishes to emote. She is not doing a very good job. Her mouth is a grim line. Her eyes drill into her own expression as if she herself might be an insurgent.

"I used to have those marks. That's why I took the Rule." Sister Josephine points at Christine's right arm in the mirror. That's not the arm Christine's tattoos are on. Christine looks down. There are purple bruises in the shape of fingerprints. Thanks, Sensei Raphael.

Christine cringes. Obviously, this woman was in a violent relationship and left it to become a Benedictine. Christine looks to the paper towel dispenser for help. She asks the dispenser how it is that she is still such an asshole. The dispenser offers nothing except a two-and-a-half inch ration of recycled paper towel. She cannot explain that she got the bruises from a sadistic loser who likes to dominate his students. What she says is, "I'm glad you are safe now. I feel honoured by your sharing that with me. Thank you."

Back at the table, Christine adjusts her chair to look away from the Benedictines and out at the pub. She makes out the back of the hot bartender going up the stairs. Glad he's not their server. Passing him coming down the stairs is Tom, dressed up, wearing a blazer, but rubbing his forehead and frowning. She raises her hand to wave him over but changes her mind when she sees a very drunk Shawna stumbling down the stairs in front of him. As she weaves her way—too quickly—toward the bottom, Shawna loses her grip on her large wine goblet. Diners pause with mouths open, forks in mid-air at the sound of shattering glass.

Shawna straightens herself up drunkenly and spots Christine. Her expression darkens. She slinks over to Christine, crunching broken glass with her stilettos. Shawna lurches into Christine and slams the table with her palms. She stoops in a half straddle over Christine, her long hair falling into Christine's face. It could be the beginnings of a grotesque lap dance, but it's not.

Shawna points a bony finger at Christine, the rest of her scantily clad body undulating in intoxication. "You're fucking him! You're fucking my husband. You're depraved! You lured him in and took him from me!"

Tom stops rubbing his forehead. The Brother stops talking, and eating, and drinking. Most of the people in the entire two floors have done the same. Even the musicians have ceased playing their lively Scottish music.

With as much Teflon as she can muster, Christine says, "Tom, make sure Shawna gets home safe, okay?"

"Oooh, don't worry about my safety. It's yours you should worry about. By the time I'm done with you, you'll be sorry. You'll be sooo sorry …"

Tom gently pulls her into his arms and slowly guides her out the door. Someone is patiently holding the door open. That someone is the hot bartender.

Shawna is almost out the door when she turns her head back with contortionist agility and screams, "I curse you, Reverend! You'll wish you were fucking spiders in hell by the time I'm done with you!" And then the bartender closes the door on Shawna and Tom, and on more curses that are now mercifully incomprehensible.

Christine feels a slight elation above her embarrassment as the hot bartender quickly strides over and squats down. Once again very close, almost in Christine's face. "I'm afraid I have to ask your party to leave."

"Right." Christine can tell that he is smelling her breath and locating her glass on the cluttered table.

The Brother is indignant. Christine briefly mistakes his quick, disgusted snort for choking. "Why? Why do we have to leave?"

"Well, I don't much enjoy being the one to inform you lot of this, but some guests are not comfortable with your choice of attire this evening."

Christine looks over at the two black-clad crows. "We haven't had dessert!" the Brother sputters. Sister Josephine is now rocking again in her chair.

The bringer of bad news now stands up and says firmly, "Not a problem, great dessert places all down this street. They need your business after the lockdown. Take some home for your people. Your meal is on the house. Let's just get a move on, shall we?"

"I don't think so. Where is the manager?" The rosy-cheeked Brother is not happy.

"I'm the manager. As a matter of fact, I'm the owner. There are people here trying to enjoy themselves." He lowers his voice slightly. "You must realize those outfits trigger a lot of survivors." Then, in a normal speaking tone, he adds, "I've had a total of three complaints this evening and now that outburst. Let me put it to you this way, Brothers and Sisters: there's no room at the inn. All right?"

Christine stands up. "Of course. We are sorry for the trouble. Thank you."

Once outside, Christine does an immediate visual search of the street, dim now that the sun is on its way down. The street-lights are on, and there's no one dangerous in the shadows, no insurgents, no Tom and Shawna. The area is clear.

In a moment, the others appear. She shakes the Brother's sweaty paw and the Sister's cool, bird-bone fingers. Sister Josephine has tears in her eyes and gently kisses Christine's bruises when she bids her farewell. Christine smiles her most brilliant, achingly false smile.

If fucking spiders in hell is all she has to worry about then she has it made in the shade. Christine has spent time in hells which makes sex with spiders a vacation.

MRS. DEE IS FILLED with the desire to call her daughter to announce that she is finally, at long last, making use of her gift. No, she must not let on that she has waited this long.

Sitting on her bed in her bathrobe, she opens the exquisite basket full of artisan beauty products. A bright selection of tiny bottles and jars are nestled into the paper straw in the basket. Almond-based gels, oils, and creams. Mrs. Dee's knuckles whiten as she grips the bottle of almond-infused bath oil. Doesn't her daughter know better than this? This obsession with almonds is killing all the bees. Which is killing the planet. Under the straw, she finds a card with a bumblebee on it.

Mrs. Dee begins to calm down as she reads that they've planted thousands of almond trees. Hmm, sustainable, ethically sourced. Right. Okay then. She sighs. Mrs. Dee has raised a good daughter.

She runs herself a bath, nice and hot, and pours in some almond oil. The smell of almonds is intoxicating and fills the ensuite Norman built for them. She sinks deeper into the lovely water, admiring the rose-shaped light fixture. He would have enjoyed some of this almond cream for his shaving, when he could still shave. That's a good idea. She'll bring some of this to the home. He still welcomes her touch. She'll massage some into his hands and feet.

Mrs. Dee must keep her eye on the time. She cannot linger too long in this bath. Today is her debut modelling for the drawing group. Evan and the others talked her into it after she finished her design for that blasted window. She borrowed a perspective trick used by Russian iconographers to have Mary's gaze nearly omnipresent. It worked out very well indeed.

The absolute nerve of the Reverend, dumping that huge responsibility on her! The drawing group had been terribly supportive. Very few people understand the suffering that making art can bring. What is remarkable is Evan's awareness of this and many other deep facets of life. At such a young age. Simply remarkable.

Mrs. Dee steps dripping from her bath, towels dry, and stands rubbing almond body cream into the flesh of her legs, her arms, and just a dab on her face.

After pulling up to the church, she notices the place is teaming with life. The grounds are filled with rodents of all sorts. In addition to the coyotes, there are now hawks and other raptors in the high trees around the graveyard. She watches a hawk plummet to a grave marker and sit there. She swallows hard. It has something under its claws. The little brown scrap wriggles and then lies still, and the hawk lifts off. Going somewhere more private to have its dinner, she suspects.

Mrs. Dee does her best to forget about all that as she empties her bladder in the dank church hall bathroom before her modelling session. It is time to forget about all annoyances. God has given her today to live, not to worry.

Because the fall day is rainy and overcast, the group has set up a powerful spotlight. The cool September air is damp and chill. As Mrs. Dee lets the sheet drop, she is pleased about the warmth this lamp throws onto her body. She is happy to be here.

Mrs. Dee basks in the warm gaze of those drawing her. She glances at Evan. She is being alighted and anointed by the gaze of the artists as they glance over her, into her. The room buzzes with a vital energy, almost as if this work is saving the world.

CHRISTINE IS DOING her best to accommodate the reporter for *Coastal Life*. They picked up on the viral water-breaking-window video and phoned last week. Mrs. Dee agreed to an interview and, of course, is now nowhere to be found.

Christine is seated in the last pew, in front of the narthex, the grand and high entrance of the church. Last month, Christine removed the lost-and-found box and the wobbly fold-up table with donation envelopes. On either side of the entrance are matching circular towers, ten metres in diameter. The southern tower houses the baptismal font. The northern tower is now a construction zone and the future home of a reconciliation room. Larry has taped up some plastic to keep the sawdust out of the church.

The *Coastal Life* interviewer opens the large church door. He is bouncing on his toes, with three different bags looped over his shoulder.

"Mr. Gallo."

"I hate to ask this, but can I use your bathroom? I came in from Langford."

"Of course. The door is on your right."

"This one?"

"No, that leads up to the choir loft and bell tower. The one beside it."

He unceremoniously drops his gear on the floor and opens the bathroom door. "Whoa—tiny! Is that the only one?"

"In this building, yes."

"Weird."

"Mmm." Christine hopes this pain in the ass will just relieve himself and get on with the bloody interview. As one of her teachers used to say, the house of God is not a urinal. She looks over at the north tower and notices a squirrel scurrying out of a hole in the sheet of construction plastic, out the front door the interviewer left open.

After using the washroom, he sits down beside her in the pew. He adjusts to face her as much as possible. He leans forward, rubbing his hands together.

"So that video—is it true that the bride was totally infertile before the waters came during her wedding?"

The waters? Holy hell. "I'm sorry, Mr. Gallo, I can't comment on anything like that."

"Call me Tim. Like what?"

"Any sort of medical or private information like that."

"Oh."

Christine waits for another question.

He recalculates. "But doesn't the church have a comment about plastic-induced sterility, or the fertility market, the adoption market?"

"The commodification of life, you mean?"

He picks up his notebook. "Yes, yes, exactly."

"Yes, I'm sure many in the church have valuable things to say about that subject. I'm afraid I am also going to decline entering into any discussion on that."

"Why?"

Christine looks up at the high ceiling over her head. "What kind of piece would you like to do? I was thinking a community relations piece." The crows and squirrels seem to be screaming at each other outside the church door.

She spots Mrs. Dee's window waiting to be installed. Larry has it ready on the floor, leaning against the wall underneath the old one with the missionary scene. Removing the old pane was more difficult than Larry thought.

"We are installing a new stained-glass window." Christine stands up and walks over to Mrs. Dee's work of art. The morning light is flowing in, and the space glows with rich oranges and reds. The journalist's expression remains neutral. Obviously, he is underwhelmed by this news.

"Who is that? Mary?"

Christine crosses her arms. "Yes, Mary—she can answer your first question about controlling life."

"What?"

"She was to be stoned to death."

"She was?"

"She was." Now he really looks at Mary. "Just the way Jesus came into the world blew apart human power systems."

"Whoa."

"Yeah, I know. Now look up. Look at what is being replaced."

His face changes from reverence to disgust. "But that's what happened."

"Yeah. That's what always happens."

"Power." He hasn't written down a thing.

"Okay, this is heavy. Let's go outside."

He looks relieved. "Yeah, okay." Together, they move toward the front door.

"What's this?" he asks.

"That's the baptismal font." The font is surrounded by handsomely carved wooden plant stands, a pot of rich red lilies vibrant against the white of jasmine.

"I can smell the oxygen coming off these plants." He takes his camera out of its bag and snaps a few photos. The curved tower wall is inlaid with many large blocks of glass. The light floods in like spotlights onto the foliage. "Is that running water in the font?"

"Yes, it is. Solar powered."

"Can I touch it?"

"Yes, go ahead."

The reporter lifts off the bamboo cover, and Christine takes it from him. The font is plain grey concrete. He peers into the water and dips his hand into it. He takes his glasses off and rubs the bridge of his nose.

"Thanks." He looks around appreciatively. "It's nice in here. Elegant."

"Yes." Christine replaces the cover. "This is the work of one of my wardens and another parishioner. They are both master gardeners."

He takes a few more photos. "I want to photograph the labyrinth."

"Sure." From the church steps, they see the scurry of animals around the labyrinth, and Christine leads him toward it, trying not to remark on all the wildlife.

"Did the Sunday schoolers make this?" he asks, shooting pictures of the uneven ground, churned up, with unsprouted seed and smelling distinctly like ... well, mouse turds.

Suddenly, the church hall door busts open and out flies a buck-naked Mrs. Dee. She cuts across the outer circuits of the labyrinth and spins around in the muddy centre, smacking at her bare arms and legs. "Get away, get away!" she cries.

A red-headed young man comes rushing out. He is visibly struggling not to laugh as he flings a sheet around her shoulders.

The reporter is getting all of this.

"Did they sting you?"

"Yes, dammit! My face!"

The rather handsome young man squats down and sticks his index finger into the muddy centre of the labyrinth. She lets him get close, very close. He makes shushing and cooing sounds as he smears mud onto her face.

"Be careful! Are the stingers out?"

He blows on her face. "Yes, Ingrid."

The photographer whispers "Who is that? Who are they?"

"That's my warden, the master gardener and creator of that window, Mrs. Dee."

"Who's that with her?"

Christine can't remember his name but knows that he is related to Mrs. Wilson. Is that Mrs. Dee's godson? The redhead helps Mrs. Dee up. She is pouting now, but contentedly. Enjoying his attention.

"So, I'm going to ask you to stop taking pictures. We might have to delete some of those."

"Uh, I don't think so."

Christine gives him a look. They are standing there staring at each other, on the verge of a showdown. Things had been going so well. Christine is about to snarl out a threat. "Mrs. Dee?" she says instead, "do you have a moment?"

The young man has already re-entered the church hall, and Mrs. Dee is about to do the same.

"This is the reporter from *Coastal Life*. I think you two spoke on the phone, to arrange the interview?"

Mrs. Dee picks up the hem of the sheet so she doesn't trip and comes over. A flushed, glowing, and very alive Mrs. Dee presents her hand to the reporter. She has two drying globs of mud on her face.

"Just call me Ingrid."

"I thought that since you are so much an integral part of this parish you could round out the interview? Speak about the points I may have missed?"

"Well, I would be delighted. Let's just introduce you first to the drawing club." She tightens the sheet around her. "Then I'll show you our environmentally responsible grounds."

THE SERVICE TO celebrate St. Francis's attempt to fix the church and his love of nature and animals is going well. Tom read out the passage in the Gospel of Matthew about being carefree as the birds. Jackie's choir is belting out "God's Heaven Is Our Earth."

Jackie's choir is spectacular. All identify as exploited female survivors from the street. All the basses, tenors, altos, and sopranos are in the choir loft behind the refurbished keyboard for the seventeen hundred and sixty pipes of the now good as new organ. No expense has been spared. The choir and organ together are filling the church with powerful gusts of healing sound. The sounds they make are almost too beautiful. Christine nearly loses it several times during the Kyrie, which they sing a cappella.

James is a prodigal pianist and organist. His parents convinced him to go into the RCMP to put bread on the table. That's where he met Jackie. He has devoted his retirement to learning and performing most of the great works. Both Jackie and James possess a deep understanding of liturgical music. Neither of them will take any money. They splurge on the choir robes. The robes are elegant, with a hint of bling.

The bishop reaches for and readjusts his hat and then holds onto the arms of his chair as James opens up the whole instrument. That, along with Jackie's sopranos, just about blows the roof of the church off.

Once the whole congregation has traipsed outside, Christine's exhilaration begins to wane. A mouse runs over her foot, and she resists punting it sky high. The vermin have become too abundant.

A bald eagle is perched up in a yellow cedar, and a Cooper's hawk is circling overhead. Larry says he saw a cougar slinking through the graveyard one night last week.

Christine watches as Mrs. Wilson trips over a brick and almost careens into Evan. She knows Mr. Fowler will be giving her an earful about the mud on his shoes.

The bishop actually needs to use his crook as a walking stick as they slip and slide their way to the centre of the labyrinth. Christine is praying that the bishop, who is near seventy, doesn't fall. They both turn to face the congregation that has gathered with them outside for the blessing. Christine sees a raptor of some sort up in a tree stomping a squirrel with its talons and pulling at the guts with its beak.

The bishop proclaims that the gathering is occurring on ancestral territories and offers thanks and then talks about the sacred journey of walking in truth.

"This is our path, to follow Jesus. To follow the truth, his truth, his path—his way." The clouds are moving in quickly, with low, very dark thunderheads. "And the way of truth is difficult for us."

Christine feels the shadow of wings cross her face, big wings, and hears the whoosh of flapping overhead. Are there any chipmunks at her feet? Best not to get in between a bird of prey and its prey.

The bishop continues. "I call upon you now to reflect on those places within where you dare not go. Those labyrinths within. Those twisted, wounded places where God's love is needed. You are not alone there. God is with you. God is with us." He dips a spray of cedar into a bucket of holy water that Christine is holding. Then he flicks drops of holy water out across the faces and heads of the crowd gathered around him

The bishop turns and dips the cedar bough into the water again, just as a bird lands on Christine's head—a considerable weight, and God, it has talons. The bishop leaves his spray in the bucket, and Mrs. Dee takes the bucket from her.

"Bishop, just what is on my head?" she asks quietly, holding herself very still. Christine can feel the bird adjusting its balance and tries to shift with it.

The bishop is perfectly calm. "Yes, it's a very regal bird. Don't worry, all is well, he's just … lovely."

Then the bird springs up and away, and Christine's head is suddenly too light. Christine holds out her hand so Mrs. Dee can pass the bucket back to her, but she doesn't. Christine steps closer to Mrs. Dee, gesturing for her to hand over the bucket. Mrs. Dee frowns and shakes her head. Christine looks over to the bishop, and he raises an eyebrow.

"Chasuble chasuble chasuble, Reverend." Mrs. Dee puts the bucket on the ground and begins to lift the white chasuble over Christine's head.

Christine feels warm liquid trickling down her forehead. Not rain, no—is it blood?

"Sorry it's not clean," the bishop says as he presses his handkerchief against her forehead. Her head is now more important than the blessing of the labyrinth. Can't he just work it in? This incident is very St. Francis.

He calls out to the crowd "Can anybody take—"

"I can take her." It's the maid of honour from the Stipenheind-Bluefield wedding.

Mrs. Dee reaches down and gathers up the folds of Christine's thin alb and strips it quickly over her head, leaving her in her black cassock. Christine wants to remark on how she doesn't need a hospital, but now the bishop is marching her toward the parking lot. Christine sees the maid of honour getting into the back of a sleek black car. As they approach the car, Christine realizes that the driver is holding the door open for her, Christine.

Christine climbs in, and the driver quickly gets behind the wheel.

"The General, I think, is closest, Patrick."

"Right, Mrs. Sterling."

Christine pulls the bishop's white handkerchief away from her scalp and examines the spots of blood dotting it. She dabs around her crown. The puncture wounds are all pretty superficial. It's not really worth a trip to the hospital. She'll get a tetanus shot, and that's probably it. She'll just get a cab back and help clean up. Christine reaches for her phone, but of course she's left it in her bedroom because the bishop hates cellphones.

"Must have happened when he took off." Christine meets the woman's rich brown eyes. "Because I felt like he was intentionally not digging his talons in." The woman adjusts a large diamond ring to face outward on her finger. "I suppose if he had really dug in, I'd be talking to you right now without much of a face, eh?"

Christine estimates about five carats are gleaming from the woman's hand. This is who the church ladies call Sterling Six Figures.

"It might have been a she." Mrs. Sterling reaches into her handbag and pulls out a scarf and offers it to Christine.

"Right. Might have been." Christine takes the scarf. Light grey cherry trees brushed on white with wisps of pink spill into her hand.

"I can't use this, Mrs. Sterling."

Mrs. Sterling squints. "Why not? It's silk. Antibacterial. I insist." With a slight movement, Mrs. Sterling pinches the tip of the bishop's blood- and snot-covered polyester handkerchief, jerks it away, and lets the thing fly out the slightly lowered window.

She closes the window, made of bulletproof glass. The thin layers of laminated polycarbonate are visible to Christine. The vehicle's selling point of superiority that says, "Yes, I'm powerful. Yes, I'm hated. And I'll go wherever the fuck I want." Fancy. Christine is enjoying this. She can tell the driver has skills. They are tearing down the road.

"Reverend, I do not want to abuse this time with you, but I have—I have a problem."

Christine cocks her head attentively. "Of course."

"I've just had my third miscarriage. It nearly killed me, all drama aside. The intrauterine insemination will not take, the in vitro fertilization is no dice either." She takes a deep breath. "I've exhausted every clinic, at home and abroad. My body is in ruins at twenty-nine."

Christine watches this woman, who could afford to buy a small country full of children, blather on. Perfectly manicured hands reach for an insulated stainless steel bottle.

"This—this is urine. I drink urine now." She takes a swig. "What's more is that I'm losing my mind. I'm homicidally jealous of women who get pregnant. Sheila Bluefield and I don't talk any more." She places the cap back onto the bottle. "I can't sleep. I'm addicted to sleeping pills. I know my husband wants to leave. He won't. He'll stay. It's my money. But he's miserable. We both are."

Now is the time to speak, except Christine has nothing.

"Mrs. Sterling, what is your first name?"

"Frances."

Okay, Frances. Same name as St. Francis. Still nothing. What does she say to someone so deep in their own misery? She's beyond reach. It's too bad. Frances is a nice person, Christine can feel it. And she's suffering intensely, that's clear.

Suddenly Long Lobes from the coffee shop jumps into Christine's mind. He tells her in his singsong voice, "Tell her like it is." No, she tells Long Lobes, I can't do that. I can't be brutally honest with this woman. An apparition of Long Lobes is now there, with them in the back of the Mercedes, holding a seven-dollar coffee. "Why else did you go through all this?" Long Lobes asks. "To be mute, to be afraid of speaking truth? Yes, you can tell her like it is. She's asking you for it."

He is nodding with a little smile of pure satisfaction on his face. His lobes swing forward slightly like pendulums.

Christine says a quick "Help me, God" to herself before she opens her mouth. She can feel the high performance suspension of the car as they fly through the regional park, a shortcut to the hospital. The driver guides the car around trees and other cars effortlessly on the narrow, winding road.

Christine tells Frances about St. Francis of Assisi renouncing everything, including clothing. Long Lobes is not impressed, and neither is Frances. Okay. Let's go. How about marriage as an ancient program to control property and breed armies and bases of taxation?

Frances likes that and gushes about Kamala Harris becoming vice president in the States. Change is coming. Change is here. Christine wraps Frances's thousand-dollar scarf around her forehead like a revolutionary. Long Lobes raises a fist. Words like consumption, heirs to plague, and repentance fly out of Christine's mouth. She calls Frances a six-figure sinner. Frances smiles like the Cheshire cat and says more like eight. Eight like eight on its side, as in infinity.

"Repentance is release," Christine explains. "Release from the bondage of what we are not. We're just love, made and named in love. Repentance is the gateway to knowing this love and to compassion—for self and others."

Frances is with her. She closes her eyes and lets out a sob. Christine continues. "That's what you want—to know your real value. Then nothing else matters: Money, no money. Children, no children."

Frances calls her Jesu Christy and then tries to play match-maker with the driver. Christine says that her vagina has grown over. No. It was seared shut when she was ordained. There had been smiting and blam! She smacks her pubic bone for emphasis. She can't believe how good it feels to be real. To be honest. She can tell Frances feels the same.

They scream-laugh until they cry. Frances offers her a cocktail. Christine tells her she's a recovered alcoholic and addict. Frances smiles and offers her some sparkling water. Maybe some urine? Christine declines with a giggle. Long Lobes salutes them both. His work here is done.

Christine feels the car doing a one-eighty. It stops on a dime. They have arrived at the General Hospital.

"You'll be all right on your own?"

"Yes. Thank you for the ride." Christine takes the scarf off her head and puts it in her pocket.

"Take care of yourself Jesu Christy. We need you in this world."

"Yes, you do the same." The driver clears his throat. He is already contravening the indicated flow of traffic by dropping her right in front of the hospital doors. Now they are categorically stopped in a no-stopping zone.

Christine leaves the luxury of the car, and the exterior glass doors of the hospital slide open with a swish into pure chaos. The entranceway between the two sets of doors has a sign asking you to wear booties. Christine's shoes are caked with mud and the box of booties is empty. She takes off her shoes and peers through the glass trying to find another box.

Christine realizes that she is wearing a long black cassock and a collar. Her socks are soaked, and she takes them off too. They'll have more booties inside. She goes to the hand station and soaks her hands in antibacterial foam.

Christine reaches for the collar to pull it off. An anguished voice pierces through the waiting room. "Reverend! Please! I don't want to die alone! I don't want to die alone!"

Christine sees an old man halfway out of a wheelchair as he gestures at her to come over. The waiting room is full. Some people are passed out in chairs. Others are pacing. The smell of intense body odour brought on by stress is overwhelming.

Christine catches a warning glare from the intake clerk on the far right. She is handed a box of booties. She takes out two. "May I proceed?" The clerk nods.

The man cries again, "I don't want to die alone!"

"I'm here. I'm here. We're all here. The nurses are—"

"They don't think I'm dying, but I'm dying." His skin is grey and yellow. His face is strained, and she hears him wheezing. "I keep telling them. They don't listen."

Christine finds his hand. It is shaking. She absorbs the signals of bodily death into her own body. "They're listening, I'm listening. They are so busy trying to help everyone. It's okay."

"I'm afraid. But I want to die. I want to die soon."

"He has gone ahead to prepare a room for you. What is your name?"

"Serge."

"Serge, you are beloved. You are being led to a lasting peace, beside still waters."

He knows the psalm. "Though I walk through the valley of the shadow of death, I will fear no evil."

"We fear no evil, because goodness and mercy are with us. God is with us. Serge, is there anything barring your journey home? Anything you need to talk about?" He shakes his head.

She looks into his faded blue eyes and holds his gaze. Her body floods with warmth. His face is so thin. "It's okay, you're okay. You are welcomed already, in comfort and love. I feel it. Can you?"

The man nods and closes his eyes. "Yes. Thank you, Reverend. Peace be with you."

A shrill voice breaks in. "Christine Wright. Christine Wright. Finish your registration." Christine turns around to see an attendant standing behind the glass. Her eyes are bulging and her shoulders are up around her ears.

"Someone from your church has faxed over all your documentation. You just need to sign these forms." The attendant slides the papers through the slot for Christine. She doesn't read them, just scans for blanks that need to be filled. Bloody hell they want an emergency contact. Can't leave that blank.

"I've been told to send you right through if you could just finish the forms please. And, put your booties on."

Christine finishes the forms, feels weird about jumping the queue and is led to a treatment room through a jam of gurneys.

"What's going on?" Christine asks, dodging wheelchairs, nurses, and equipment.

"Nothing," the attendant says. "This is addiction. Opioids, heroin, fentanyl, and alcohol mostly. Most ambulance calls and walk-ins are directly connected to addiction. There is very little we can do." Christine knows about this. Anyone who ends up in AA or NA knows about this but doesn't like to see it. She looks away from the gurneys to see a doctor and who must be an intern waiting outside a private treatment room. She feels special until she sees the biohazard sign on the door.

The doctor quickly examines Christine's head wounds. "Hello,

I'm Dr. Russel. It's important to move as fast as possible when birds of prey are involved. Especially when their talons are involved. Do you have any allergies?"

"None, doctor."

"Right. Good. We'll go with an intramuscular shot of anti-biotic."

"That sounds good." Christine thinks of Frances. "Am I contagious?"

The doctor looks to the intern, allowing him to answer.

"No. But has anyone touched your wounds?"

"No, no one has. Doctor …" She puts a hand on the silken, cherry orchard scarf in her pocket. The intern's eyes smile at her above his mask. "You can just call me Simon."

"Right," says Dr. Russel. "Let's get you treated. Nurse will be in soon." He puts her chart on the counter and leaves. "You are in good hands."

"Thank you both."

Christine begins to worry after half an hour passes. What's taking so long? Finally, a masked and gloved Shawna opens the door. To Christine's relief, there is a nursing student with her. Shawna talks the nursing student through administering the shot into Christine's backside and then the nursing student leaves.

Shawna waits for the door to close and takes off her mask. Shawna doesn't entirely look like Shawna. Christine has seen this before. On suicide bombers. Cue the psycho music.

Shawna's arms are rigid as she takes out another needle filled with yellow liquid from her pocket. Shawna is not under her own power. Her pupils are small, her face frozen.

"Tell me where the fuck Terry is."

"How would I know? Put that down, Shawna."

Christine can't move. Well, she can, but only in slo-mo.

"What's the matter? Ms. Fucking Holy and Shit can't move?"

No, she can't. What the hell was in that shot?

"I don't want to do this, but now the mob is looking at me for money, and I don't have it. Terry has it, I know it. They're threatening me, they're threatening Terrine, so just fucking tell me."

"Shawna—"

"I don't have time for this. You think I'm bluffing? I'm not bluffing. This should get you talking." With a fierce jab into Christine's arm, Shawna empties the syringe into her. "Where the fuck is he? Fucking tell me!"

An unwanted wash of friendliness comes over Christine. Must be sodium thiopental, a version of truth serum. There's something else in with it. Christine was familiarized with chemical torture methods in her training. They train you by shooting you full of different things. Fun for an addict—but not really. Fun and not fun all rolled into one. She knows what to expect.

Truth serums are a myth. Comfort, more friendliness, and euphoria begin to flood Christine. Big deal. The only truth she's connecting with is how embarrassing this is. Here is Shawna in her scrubs with little puppy dogs wearing bow ties. Christine paralyzed and completely prone with bird talon scratches all over her head. No one is going to find out about this.

"Code white, code blanc. Code white, code blanc," is announced over the hospital public address system. Hm. The discrete hospital code for aggression. Would stabbing this bitch in the eye with a hypodermic qualify?

Simon comes in with a wheelchair. Shawna quickly remasks her face while her back is to the door. "Doctor?"

"The emergency has been closed. All our security guards and porters are busy right now. Nurse you're needed at your station. I'll escort our Reverend out."

Shawna leaves and Simon helps her get out of her chair and into the wheelchair. Simon seems a little surprised by how much of her weight he has to take.

"Someone pulled out a toy gun. They look so real. The SWAT team is still here. Let's get you to another exit."

He avoids the circus of Emergency and wheels her to a side entrance. She can't tell him what's just happened. Too embarrassing. All will be well. They pass through an underground tunnel, rolling by garbage bins and a few maintenance people on their break. When they are out through a side door, he calls a taxi and waits with her. Christine is silent. She's getting nervous. Shawna gave her a huge dose. It'll wear off.

As Simon gets her on her feet and is guiding her toward the open taxi door, her knees buckle.

"Reverend. Reverend? Oh my God."

He takes her pulse. She's back in the wheelchair. Simon is now sprinting the wheelchair back through the tunnel. Her cassock flies up over her head. Simon screeches to a halt and whips his cellphone out. "Fuck, no signal." He pushes her at a full run and then screeches to another halt beside an intercom dating from the cold war from the looks of it. Simon pounds the button. Nothing. "Code blue code blue code blue, motherfucker!" He sees a fire alarm and reaches for it.

"Simon."

"What!"

"Simon. Calm the fuck down. You're gonna give me a heart attack." Christine starts laughing and winces, holding her left shoulder. The pain is excruciating. "Don't pull that. It'll shut the building down. Just get me back. You can do it. Let's go."

"Okay okay okay okay. Code blue code blue. Let's go. Okay. Okay."

The world goes a funny white colour as she fades in and out. "This is fun, Simon," she slurs. "Faster!" She almost laughs.

In some treatment room now, lots of noise and yakking over her. Are they cutting off her cassock? An IV appears in her arm.

"Her vitals, doctor—"

"Acknowledged." It's Dr. Russel. Christine relaxes.

"Is this thing even on?" That's not relaxing whatsoever. She holds her breath. Is there breath?

"Doctor!"

"I know! I know! I see it too!"

"That doesn't make any sense! This isn't right. This isn't right!"

Great. They've discovered she has no heart.

"Stop the epinephrine! I said stop!"

Then there is a long pause.

"Inducing coma now."

AFTER AN UNKNOWN TIME, a handsome fox is holding her hand. The fox speaks.

"Don't talk. Don't talk. Here, here. Take a sip. They've just pulled I don't know how many tubes out of your throat."

"You sound like Joey." Christine's voice is as hoarse as a drunken, chain-smoking grandma.

The fox in a sharp blue blazer laughs. "It is Joey, hon. Have another sip. The doctors woke you up because they need to talk to you."

"You look nice. You look very handsome." Christine likes the way his paw feels on her hand.

"Thanks, sweetie. I was on a date. I didn't know I was your emergency contact—"

"You're all I got, Joe—"

Three little pigs saunter into the room.

"Ms. Wright. Emergency Director of Care, Michael Nichols, and you know Dr. Russel."

"Mr. Nichols, she's a Reverend," says a little piggy holding a clipboard that sounds like Simon.

"Right you are. And you also know Dr. Field. Nice to see you on the other side of that, Reverend. We need to have an important conversation. Some events have occurred, and we need your legal consent to continue." Christine doesn't much care for this piggy. "It has come to our attention that the nurse who administered your treatments knowingly altered the compounds, which caused, ah, a number of medical emergencies. She has been taken into custody."

"Naughty, naughty."

"Yes, indeed. That being said, she has confessed and supplied Dr. Russel with the compounds that you were injected with."

Dr. Russel takes over. Christine much prefers this piggy. His white coat goes well with his light pink skin. So cute, so innocent. Christine feels immense guilt over all the bacon she has ever ingested.

"Christine, I had to induce a coma to buy enough time to figure this out. Your toxicology doesn't help us, and I don't trust the nurse's account."

The director piggy says, "We need your instructions on how to proceed and your signature."

"Dr. Russel?" Drunken grandma speaks.

"Yes?"

"What would you do?"

This little piggy pushes his glasses back up his snout. "You're a fit, healthy, and strong forty-year-old woman. I would let us keep your fluids up and allow your system to respond. Comas can be tricky in my opinion. So can introducing any further compounds."

"Yeah, let's just let it ride."

"So, she is electing no further treatment. That's the bottom option." Director piggy points to the clipboard the third little piggy is holding.

Clipboard piggy brings over the form. He has a really curly tail. His eyes are like an emoji.

"Simon, is that you?" Christine signs the third option. She is a tiger. A white tiger. She admires her striped arm. She wonders if she is a lady tiger. She gives Simon the pen back and reaches her paw down between her legs. Yes, she is a lady tiger. Simon piggy waits for her to stop pawing her crotch before he fastens a restraint to her wrist and anchors that to the bed. She doesn't mind. It's comfy.

"Yes, Christine, it's Simon. So glad you are still here with us."

"Christine, you might notice a strong feeling of euphoria. That's the ketamine. The amount administered, if we are to trust the nurse's account, is enough to sedate a small village. The stimulant we used to rouse you is the gentlest possible, but I'm just informing you that you've been restrained for your own protection. The restraints will be removed as soon as possible."

The sly fox snickers. "You are going to need something a little stronger than these to hold her. I'm not kidding."

The doctors leave and eventually so does Joey. After a while, she gets wheeled into a different room. It's quiet and soothing, but she doesn't like it. There is a darkness crouching somewhere in this new room. It waits patiently.

The darkness rises up like a flood, surging out from under the bed and flowing over her. She is under, and staying under. And there's nothing she can do about it.

EVENTUALLY the restraints are taken away and the IV removed. After a week, Joey returns, no longer a fox. Time to go home. He brings her some new underwear, jeans, a T-shirt, and a nice trench.

"These aren't mine."

"I know, but they are now. You're welcome. There's media outside."

"What?"

"Oh yes. Yes, indeed. But I know what to do. The Mini is parked at the secret entrance." He pulls out aviators. "Put these on."

The red Mini is a convertible. Joey enjoys taking his lover of the month along with his little dog on scenic drives. Joey has his little rocket fired up, in first gear, and on the road to the church just as she's buckling her seatbelt.

Joey looks over at her and smiles. "I put the top up. You know, in case that bird comes back."

"Thanks, Joey."

"Did it hurt? You know. When it landed on you?"

"No. It was heavy though. I think it was being careful."

"The bishop said it was a peregrine falcon. Really bushy legs, looked him right in the eye. It was in his sermon on Sunday. It really moved him."

"Oh." Christine can't stand the idea of being the focus of this kind of attention. She pulls the mirror down.

The talon marks will scar. They are delicate, almost like razor cuts. She looks into her own eyes. What's different? Physically she feels not too bad. The hospital spared no effort.

Mrs. Dee says a quick hello in the church parking lot. No media here. The attention must just be focused on the hospital. Or on Shawna. Mrs. Dee reaches out and warmly squeezes Christine's elbow. "Some very large military men came by. They said they were your friends." Mrs. Dee's tone is soft. "There's been a few changes made to your residence. I've stocked your fridge. Please let me know if there is anything you need."

It seems as though all that was required for Mrs. Dee and Christine to get along was an attempt on her life by Nurse Shawna.

Christine invites Joey in and goes upstairs to get her phone. There it is, charging on her desk by her bed where she left it over a week ago. She picks it up. No calls. Ouch. Two photos pop up in a text bubble. The first is of the lower left-hand side of her closet. The second is of two guys wearing balaclavas standing by the desk she now stands at. One of them is sniffing her chair. It's two guys from her team. What's left of the team. They must have heard about what happened on the news.

Christine goes to the closet and lifts what she thinks is the right floorboard. There is a tricked out Beretta APX with a silencer beside it. It's custom. The grips are an iridescent pearl pink. She laughs. It's a good joke. She wonders where the ammo is. Christine puts the floorboard back and returns to her phone. There's a new app shaped like a shield on the screen.

She comes back down the stairs and tries out the app. There is only on and off. She hits on and hears iron sliding across the doors and windows. The old house shudders slightly.

"A gift from your friends?" Joey has put the kettle on. Something is not right with him.

"Yes. Well, I wouldn't call them friends."

"What do you call people who care about you? What do you call me? Am I your friend?"

"Well, not really. You're a mentor. These guys were on my team. When I was in Afghanistan. When I—" Christine stops. That's enough. She's very tired. Joey notices.

"I don't think you'll be seeing Shawna again."

"No."

"They are going to make an example of her. Not exactly what the health care system needs right now."

"Right."

"After all they've been through."

Joey doesn't normally discuss current affairs or make small talk.

"So, the bishop presided last Sunday when you were in the hospital. I came. He's a good preacher, eh?"

"Yes." Christine busies herself laying out teacups, milk, and sugar.

"Your organ is dynamite, and that choir is, well, heavenly. I've never heard anything quite so beautiful. I forgot that about your denomination. Hypnotic. Seductive."

"That's Jackie from the RCMP depot. That's her choir. She works with the exploited."

"And on organ?"

"That's James, her husband. He's a retired profiler."

"Quite the duo."

"Quite the duo." Christine pours Joey's tea exactly how he likes it. Three quarters of a tablespoon of sugar and ten percent cream until it's the colour of finished pine. She has to switch arms. Her shoulder can no longer handle the weight of a teapot.

Joey has been far too nice. Something is going on.

"What's up, Joey?"

"I don't want to upset you. You need calm after what's happened."

"What—that? That was a speed bump. Come on." Christine takes a sip of hot tea. She knows what's coming is not good at all.

"I'm going into community. My application has been approved."

Christine slides the cookies over to him. "Congratulations. I'm happy for you."

Joey selects one and takes a quick nibble. His pinky is outstretched. "No, you're not. You're devastated. I know you are. You told me in the hospital that I'm all you have."

So she did. Silly tiger. "I don't know what you want me to say."

Joey slams his fist down on the table. Some of his tea spills. His cookie crumbles. "Goddammit, Christine, I want you to start telling the truth! That's all I've ever asked of you."

Christine puts her tea down. She exhales. Again with this. She'll gladly take another round with Shawna over Joey when he gets like this.

"You told me you left the Church right before they were about to devour you."

"Yeah, I did, wanna see the bite marks? Vicious!"

"And so what is this? What the fuck, Joey!"

"I'm bored. You can't beat the drama. It's like being in all of Shakespeare's plays at once. Throw in a few Greek tragedies too. What can I say, besides, you're not upset because of me."

"I know." Christine sighs. "This is about me."

"If you cannot be yourself, who else will you be?"

"Okay, fine. I don't know why you would do this. They are beneath you, those people I met. They want to use you. I need you. I don't have ... I don't have anyone."

"Oh, there we go. Poor little orphan Chrissy."

"I am an orphan, remember?"

Joey does a long blink. "Right. So ... what?"

"So, I really don't have ..."

"You see, that's the bullshit right there. Anyone else looking at your life right now would see success, Christine. The military throws money and medals at you. This parish is a triumph. Your bishop sings your praises because of what's happening at your church. These 'teammates' just fortified this house for you. "

"Well, that's not me."

Joey was not finished and is now even angrier. "Your humility has always needed work, Christine. You go and cut yourself off all the time. From yourself. From other people. From God. Christine, there's humble, and then there's pathetic. Do you know the difference?"

"Yes."

Joey holds her in a long and full pause. "You see, I don't think you do. Real humility knows strength. But you, you don't see it that way. There is an apathy at work in you."

"Joey, don't."

"Don't what? Speak the truth?"

"It's easier."

"Than what?"

"Than being alive."

"That is the biggest load of horseshit and you know it! Oh, behold, we are in the very presence of the immaculate martyr. Oh, woe is Christine. Listen, I was there before they pulled you out of that coma, and I've got news for you." Joey collects his crumbs and sops up the spilled tea with his napkin. When he is finished, he looks her dead in the eye. "That Nurse What'shername—Shawna? Well, the Devil himself thrust his hand up Nurse Shawna's backside and waltzed her into the dispensary. She killed you. She killed you three or four times over by what the entire staff of that hospital had to say."

"I know."

Joey jumps up from his chair. "What? You knew? Oh my god. Christine, you are unbelievable!"

Christine swallows. Tears are coming soon, but not yet. "Well, I didn't know. I just could feel her hate. It was palpable. I'm fucking used to it by now."

Joey sits back down. "You were saved, Christine. And we both know this isn't the first time."

Christine shakes her head. A few tears burn their way down her cheeks. She is slumped over in a defensive posture. Can't sob, must not sob.

"Why were you saved, Christine? Tell me that. Why? Why? So you could throw your life away? So you could sit there and let Shawna do that to you?"

Christine doesn't know why she was saved. She has never known. Why did she survive the car crash that took her family out? Why did she live through Afghanistan? Why didn't her suicide work? Why didn't Shawna's caustic cocktail finish her?

"I don't know! I don't deserve these second chances! God is torturing me!"

"Like God doesn't have better things to do than torture you. Okay, yes, Divine Intelligence of the Universe, let's give this girl life, a really nice life—oh, there she goes with the vodka. Oh dear. Okay, let's try again. Oh, there she goes dismantling bombs and shit. Oh well, we tried." Joey pours himself another cup. "You know what your problem is, Christine?" Christine braces herself. "You are God's spoiled little princess. Every time you don't get your way, you have a little suicidal temper tantrum. Wahhh wahhh."

The crying begins. Christine fights it, trying to keep a straight face.

"For the love of Mary, do you know how ugly that is? It's like a cat choking on a hairball. Just cry, Christine. Let's get this show on the road." Joey taps his watch. "Tick-tock. Time to get human. Let's get our human on!"

Christine does get the show on the road. She cries. She howls. She wails. She screams. Joey matches her.

"The guys think I can't take care of myselllf!"

"Well, you sort of donnn't."

"Everyone hates meee!"

"Not everyyyone."

This goes on for some time until they are both spent.

"I haven't had sex in eight years," Christine says softly.

"What? Well, that's your problem right there." He picks up another cookie. Mrs. Dee would approve. He is, after all, a guest. "Easy fix." Christine rolls her red eyes at him and blows her nose. "What? I'm serious!" Joey says.

"Like having sex with someone is going to fix everything."

"Well, God knows my bag of tricks is empty. Your self-imposed exile from the human race must end, Christine. You do know this, don't you?"

"It's not self-imposed."

"Oh, really? Who then? Who is it that banished you? Don't say God because the Creator just keeps pulling you back in. I mean, it's like a Godfather movie with you."

"Okay, well—"

"When in doubt, resort to metaphysics, or better yet metaphor—"

"Joey, I really don't think—"

"Intercourse, Christine. Lengthy, intense intercourse—"

"So that will—"

"And like sixty-nine for a good long while—"

"Joey—"

"Interpenetration. As much of it as possible. Every orifice. Any place moist, in case you forgot. At least now you have some privacy, for God's sake, thanks to that shield thingy. Just, you know, lock up the batcave and have at it. It'll be easier without the entire parish traipsing in here all the bloody time."

Joey puts his cookie down and starts making obscene gestures with his hands.

"I don't—"

"Fuse. You need to fuse. Fusion. Hot hot hot fusion with another human being."

"Okay, okay enough—"

"No, not enough. More. Now. Immediately. Or as soon as possible. You know, let me finish this cookie and maybe let your head heal. Actually, you're looking pretty rough. All this murder and revenge and mayhem. Might want to hit the spa. For like a month." Joey snorts.

Christine closes the cookie tin. Joey opens the fridge door and inspects, giving a murmur of approval. He closes the fridge, makes his way to the front door, and puts his coat on.

Christine opens the door for him. Joey's eyes give her a thorough once-over and then a wink.

"Shouldn't be hard for you. To hook up. You are what my mother would have called a real looker."

Christine is slouched against the door frame.

"Don't worry, my dear, you have me until next week. I'll tell you what, we'll have you over to ours for supper, all right? And make sure you get to a meeting. All those drugs! Isn't ketamine a pricey high-end grade of street drug? You got the good stuff in there, that's for sure. Silver lining. Just saying."

"Joey."

"Christine."

"Why do I have to go through all of this? I'm not playing Pollyanna here, I really don't know."

"I know. I know." Joey puts his hand over Christine's heart. "I know something is broken in there. Like really fucking broken, like someone threw the most delicate clock onto the tile floor."

"Jesus, Joey."

"From a ladder."

"Just put me out of my misery, would you?"

He puts his ear on her chest. "But it is being repaired. I know it. I can hear it." He lingers there, listening, and then lets out a little sigh. He pulls back and puts an arm on each of her shoulders. "The answer, Christine, is simple, but not easy. We are made from love to love and be loved." And with that Joey turns around and walks down the path to the parking lot.

He begins to hum a little as he makes his way back to his Mini. She wonders if he'll get rid of his car when he joins. No, it's doubtful. Joey won't be giving up his drives. He'll be back, or he'll be gone somewhere else. Joey cannot be tamed. He's got better things to do than to be a circus act for the living dead. He is as wild as they come. Joey is like the wind.

Leaves are already falling. Big red maple and yellow alder leaves line Joey's path. Christine loves this time of year. Autumn is when she was born. She recalls her last birthday before the accident, when she turned eleven. She hears them singing to her and sees the burning candles. Enough.

She closes the door, pulls out her phone, and barricades herself in. She likes the clickety-clack the barricades make.

Christine makes her way upstairs. She notices the towel rack has been fixed. Time to sleep in her own bed. Joey is correct about the whole love thing. Christine has always empirically known this truth about love—that's all we are here for. She was hoping for a different answer because she can't feel it, or hasn't in a long time. She looks at her bed. It looks completely different. It's more like a five-star hotel bed.

She pulls the curtains closed and takes all her new clothes off, folding them carefully. Mrs. Dee must have bought her new bed sheets, and this duvet. Nice. She pulls the covers back and climbs in. It is over-the-top luxury. She puts her head down on a lofty pillow. There is something underneath it.

Her hand discovers the ammo under the pillow. A lot of it. Christine feels under the other pillow. More of the same. About twenty boxes. Christine climbs back out of bed and goes to her closet.

She squats down, removes the floorboard, and picks up the weapon. Very nice. It's almost the colour of rose quartz. Christine climbs back into bed, selects a box of hollow points, fills a clip, and inserts it. Christine then pulls her duvet back up around her and lies down.

The air in the house is cool. The high thread count sheets feel sweet on Christine's skin. Mrs. Dee has tucked everything way too tight. It's like she is being held down. Christine kicks out all the sheets from the edges. The duvet is free now and lofts overtop without restriction.

Christine turns onto her side and nestles her head back into her pillow. She presses her head down until she feels the shape of the ammunition boxes underneath. Joey can leave her. She'll be fine.

It takes some time, but God's little princess eventually finds the perfect position and falls into a deep sleep with both hands wrapped around the loaded weapon.

THE DOOR ALARM at Priceless Memories sounds bored. "Bong-bong, another loser just entered your store. Bong-bong, this store is filled with garbage," it says.

Seth waits for the years of filth and dust to reach his nose after the door closes behind him. How do these places stay open by selling people's discarded junk? Seth knows how they stay open. By stealing, that's how. But not on Seth's watch.

"That you, Seth?"

"Yeah, it's me, Dwight."

As he waits for Dwight to call him back, he scans the shelves for any new worthwhile additions. He quickly makes his way over to the medals. Dwight has already removed them, as expected. Fucking dirty thief. Dwight has figured out when Seth is likely to drop in.

Now that Seth's retired, he could switch things up if he wanted. Stop giving Dwight any courtesy and start paying surprise visits, catching Dwight with his medals out. These creeps, they tell widows that the medals are worthless and then they sell for a lot of money. He even has the time now to park outside, waiting and watching. Hold watch over this dirty fucking swindler.

No, his system is better. This is how he and his dad used to do it. His dad told him, the first thing you do is you get to know the store owner and establish a relationship. This involves a lot of talking, or rather, listening. The trick is to get the store owner to start talking about themselves. About their business. That way you can—casually, eventually—find out who the medal belonged to. Get it back to the family or the regiment. Get it back where it belongs. That's a job well done. That's how he used to spend time with his dad. Pensioners pawn their best things after Thanksgiving to free up some money for Christmas.

"Come on back, Seth."

Seth makes his way past the LPs, furs, lamps, jewellery, watches, silverware, a stuffed eagle, lots of crystal, and dolls. Unblinking porcelain eyes watch as Seth tries to sidle by with as little contact, as little contamination as possible.

Dwight, a huge, bearded man with thick labourer's hands, is sitting down at his workbench. The floor is covered in sawdust, and the room is filled with half-done repairs. Seth smells polish. Good fucking luck polishing any of this shit.

Dwight's work light is on, and he is wearing high-powered magnifying glasses. They fasten to his head like goggles. Being about one hundred and fifty pounds overweight, he has raised his worktable to clear his bulging gut. His shit locker. Otherwise, his arms wouldn't be able to reach what he is working on. Dwight doesn't bathe much—he's the kind of man who sports the greasy-hair look. Dwight's married. Seth has never met the woman, but Dwight's wearing work pants and a plaid flannel shirt that most likely have never been washed. So the missus is not much for washing machines.

Seth begins to wonder about Dwight's underwear and quickly decides to stop thinking about that. It triggers the horror of basic training, when he had to use the same washing machine as every-one else in the platoon. That was the worst torture. Not getting screamed at, being frozen, exhausted, punished, or terrified. No. It was knowing that his underwear was being washed with every other Tom, Dick, and Harry's.

As soon as Seth could afford it on his meagre paycheque, he

bought the very top-of-the-line washer and dryer. Front load. Steam-clean cycle. He replaces them every five years. Worth every penny. He relaxes a little just thinking about the beep the machine makes when the cycle is done. Sort of like the chimes in casinos. Very soothing. They inform him that his textiles are clean and sterile. That's how he wants things.

What is Dwight working on under his light? It's a sparkling diamond ring that glints as he moves it in his paw-like hands. The goggles give Dwight an air of trade proficiency, although the only thing he's proficient in as far as Seth is concerned is mouth breathing.

Seth can't look at him any more. He glances up past him, and something catches his eye. It's the blackened candlestick he last saw in Wright's office, along with its matching partner. Unbelievable. He has to get a closer look.

"What do we have here, Dwight?"

Dwight follows Seth's gaze. "Those, my friend, are my retirement fund. Just waiting for pickup by armoured car."

"Sold?"

"No. But will be soon. Safer to have them locked up while the dealers deal."

"May I?" Seth puts his hand on the worklight handle.

"Yeah. Knock yourself out." Dwight puts the ring down, stands up, and pulls his chair aside to look along with Seth at the sticks.

"You want to sit down, Seth?"

"No, no. I'm good. Good day today. Thanks, Dwight." Dwight points the light at the sticks.

"Wow, what happened to this one? Can I pick it up?"

"Yeah, sure. I bought them at a rummage sale at the convent there. Those crazy hags. A young one sold them to me. They don't wear their outfits any more. Yeah it's a shame about the black one." Dwight takes off the high-powered glasses and stashes the ring in a drawer.

"So they've been valued then, eh?"

"That's right. That's why I'm paying for proper storage until they're sold. With the damage, its only half a million. Would have been one or even two million otherwise."

"Two million? For some religious knick-knack? That's crazy." Seth can't take his eyes off the black one. It's like it's calling out to him. "Do you mind? I want to take a closer look."

"Sure." Dwight hands him the glasses.

Seth picks up the black stick. He knows what he's holding. He's holding his destiny. He's been sent here. To find this.

On the bottom, the edge of a velvet foot pad has curled up just enough to reveal the metal underneath. There's blood there. He can pretty much smell it. That's blood. This is a fucking murder weapon. This is her murder weapon. That smug bitch. This is too good to be true.

"Yeah, that's the hallmark underneath there. From England apparently. Norwich."

Seth quickly sanitizes the glasses with his disposable wipes. He blows on the alcohol to dry it. He can hear his own heartbeat over Dwight's mouth breathing. He gets the glasses on and his eyes adjust. Sure enough, on the bottom, under the edge of a torn velvet foot pad, there is some dried blood.

His eyes move up to where the candle plugs into the holder; it's less ornate, a smoother surface. The glasses make him feel a little unsteady. He spots a thumb and index fingerprint in a specific configuration. This candlestick was definitely used as a weapon.

It's like the prints were cooked into the metal. They are slightly raised. He adjusts the light and brings the stick up close. The corrosion that chloride ions cause on metal from the salt in sweat has been increased somehow. It's like the same process for pulling prints off shell casings. These prints will never go away. The only way now is to actually take the surface layer of the metal right off.

Seth steadies himself and takes a closer look. Is this a joke? He moves the stick back and forth slightly, letting the prints fall into the sharpest spot. His heart is beating so loudly he wonders if Dwight can hear it.

Sure enough, the prints appear like a patchwork quilt. He sees lines of scars breaking up the normal swirl. Prints like what Frankenstein's monster would have. These are Wright's prints.

"I'll give you eight hundred thousand." Seth takes the glasses off.

Dwight's mouth breathing stops momentarily and then resumes. "Nine."

Seth shouldn't be surprised by this asshole gouging him. "Nine it is." Why not? He's not going to live to spend his retirement money anyway. He's doing better than his parents. Neither lived to see retirement. Obviously, this is what he is supposed to do with it. He's not a religious man, but this is a miracle. He's just experienced a miracle in this filthy junk pit.

"Sold."

Seth reaches out and shakes Dwight's hand. He stops himself from immediately pulling out another wipe to clean his hands. He knows his behaviour sometimes makes him seem crazy. Seth isn't crazy, he just doesn't like touching people. Besides, he has hand sanitizer in the truck.

"I need more than a handshake, Seth."

"I'll go to my bank."

"It's after five."

"Right. Shouldn't take more than a few days." He gives Dwight his goggles back and starts making his way out. He pauses at the door and calls back to Dwight. "I want them as is, Dwight. That's important. Just like they are now. Understood?" Seth hears Dwight grunt a yes before he leaves, touching the door handle with as little hand surface area as possible.

The just-as-bored-sounding alarm marks Seth's exit. "Bong-bong, the clean freak is gone."

When Seth leaves, he can't help himself. He finds a vantage point where he can spy on Dwight over in the next doorway beside one of Priceless Memories' bay windows. As he squats down, he notices junkies have left piss and other mess the rest of society is supposed to clean up. His thighs and lower back are tight and sore.

Sure enough, the big bulk of Dwight appears. He's got the military medals with him, on a jewellery display pad. As Dwight moseys toward the front of the store to place them back in a display cabinet, the sun hits the medals and both Seth and Dwight see they are thick with dust. Seth can see the dust from here. That lazy fuck, he's never cleaned them. Seth watches as Dwight tries to blow the dust off them. The dust won't budge. Determined, Dwight blows again, and Seth watches as the sunbeam showcases Dwight's spit spraying all over them.

CHRISTINE HAS ALREADY performed the consecration. It's Thanksgiving Sunday, and it's standing room only in the church. All the folded chairs are out—they will have to buy more in the coming days.

The sun rises later every day. Christine doesn't mind. She doesn't mind the rain either. Mrs. Dee's window shines brightly with the slanted light that comes in fall. The clouds moved in and made their seal over the sky during the prayers for the people. The thick, dark layer burst open, and the rain was heavy.

The choir has paused. The servers are all on their knees. So is everyone else who chooses to be. The thurifer swings the thurible wide. The sanctuary is smoky with incense.

Brought out only on special days, it emits a blend of frankincense, myrrh, benzoin, and storax. The fragrance holds the wisdom of the ages, working beyond the auric field. Christine raises the gifts of God high above her head and presents them.

Instead of the resounding call of human thankfulness and Tom ringing the bell, there is another sound. Like the snarling of a wild animal that is cornered. Christine hands the sacrament over to one of her honorary priests, a retired clergyperson who still wishes to serve.

"Do you want me to come?" Tom whispers.

"No, it's fine. Make sure Suze and Deb get the gluten-free?"

Tom nods and Christine skirts around the sanctuary and steps out the door to the office. As she makes her way through the office toward the rear office door, the snarling grows more fierce. A powerful dog or a wolf is killing something.

As Christine opens the office door, she mentally checks off that all the dogs that come with owners to services are inside. Mr. Poncho and Muffin.

Christine sees an older couple watching a sweet-looking retriever in the labyrinth. It has a rabbit in its jaws and is shaking it back and forth. Finishing it off.

The man says, "Good boy. You kill it."

The woman says, "That's right, baby boy. You got it."

Horror grips Christine. It's her foster parents, the people who took the tragedy of losing her family and turned it into hell. After all this time she never thought her foster parents would be obscene enough to ever contact her again.

They don't merit that title. Pedophile and accomplice would be more accurate. They are working the dog into a frenzy with their praise. There is bloodlust in the centre of the labyrinth.

Eighteen children are gathered with Ananda, the woman Mrs. Dee has finally stopped calling the witch, in the church hall right now for their pageant "auditions." They have enough children now for a Sunday school. Its first public event will be at Christmas with a nativity pageant.

Christine can't stand the idea of predators being so close to the children right now. She hurries toward the couple and their dog.

"You and that dog need to be gone in about two minutes."

"Christine! Look dear, it's Christine. I told ya. We saw you in the paper and wanted to come wish you happy birthday."

Christine isn't going to talk any more. She's going to do something else. Something final. Something she should have done long ago.

There's a tarp in the shed big enough to cover their bodies. She'll grab it on the way back after she gets the weapon. Time to move. Christine sprints for the residence. There is more than enough time to get the Barretta and end this chapter once and for all.

Christine trips and falls flat on her face on top of Terry's grave. She feels Terry's hand gripping her ankle.

"Oh, darlin', you okay? Go over there and help her up, would you?"

As Christine scrambles to her feet, she sees the pedophile walking steadily toward her across the graves. She makes it to her door, and she's fiddling with her phone, looking for the shield app. Where the hell is it?

"Did you not hear the Reverend?" a booming voice calls out. Is that a Scottish accent? "She's asked you to leave."

"Who are you? Just stay out of this. This is a family visit, that's all. We've driven a ways." The sound of that man's voice hits Christine and she lurches forward and throws up into a rhododendron. Between the mud and the vomit, the chasuble is done.

The Scot's clothing is quickly getting wet. Only Special Operations types wear wet clothing the way he does now. "It doesn't appear like she's in the mood for a visit, does it?"

Christine finds the shield app and opens the house. She looks at the barman with his Special Forces chest. "They have to go," she insists.

Once inside, Christine activates the barricade. She slumps down against the front door. Adrenaline is still surging through her. She has the acid of bile in the back of her throat.

There's more. Christine races upstairs. She gets to the toilet just in time.

She fills a glass of water and rinses her mouth, then takes the chasuble off and leaves it in a messy heap on the bedroom floor.

Christine looks out the bedroom window and sees an RV turn out of the lot. Back in the bathroom, her body decides there is more that needs to be expelled.

Tom sends her a text. "Good?" He's worried because she's not back.

"Yes sry plz do dismissal. No coffee hour parish supper 2nite"

A soaked Scot is at her front door when she opens it, his hand held up as if to knock.

"They're gone, and so is the dog." He comes up on the stoop to get out of the rain. He realizes he is too close and steps back down. Christine stands aside.

He comes in and immediately takes his boots off. "Sorry, you didn't invite me in." He starts to put them back on again.

Christine shakes her head. "No, it's fine. Come in. Come in. I mean it." She barricades the house again. The sound of steel shimmying down does not seem to faze the Scot. "I'll be right back." She runs upstairs, fetches him a towel, and takes it down to him. He stands there drying himself off, a golden ratio of strength, height, and looks.

"What brings you by today? Did you come for the service, sorry, what's your name?"

"Nathan. This is a nice house. Reminds me a little of home." He looks cold.

"Nathan from The Scot's Caber. Yes, I'm Christine, the escapee from the looney bin." Christine tilts her head back and flashes a big smile at him. She catches that wide-open look in his eyes again. "Please sit down and make yourself comfortable, I'll put the kettle on. Go ahead and make the fire."

Christine takes her boots off, puts the kettle on, and then runs back upstairs. Off comes the cassock and collar. Christine has a quick shower, brushes her teeth, throws on the jeans and T-shirt Joey got her, and comes back down just as the water boils. There is some time to talk. Mrs. Dee and Mrs. Wilson are busy in the hall and in their glory. Finally, all the linens, plates, and table settings are being used. For only the second time, the supper—for close to a hundred people—will be held not in her residence but in the church hall.

After Christine serves Nathan his tea, they sit back in their chairs by the fire. She has a few hours before she needs to show up and help with the supper set up.

"Right. Well, the article."

"The article. What article is that?"

"The one in *Coastal Life*."

Christine had completely forgotten about it. "Ah." Great. Here we go.

"You're Christine Wright. Or Sergeant Wright."

"Um, right."

"Well, your rank wasn't in the article. But your Victoria Cross was."

Christine chokes on her tea and sprays it all over her T-shirt. God damn that Mrs. Dee. Nothing about an old lady running around naked with a young man—oh no. "I really wish they hadn't of printed that."

"Yeah I get it. Well, I'm RRS, or I was."

Royal Regiment of Scotland. Christine's eyes brim up with hot tears. Her throat is swelling.

"I was there," he continues. "My team was there. If it weren't for you and your guys, well, we both know what would have happened. I ... Well, when I found out, I wanted to thank you in person. For what you did."

"Oh my God. Whew. I'm so sorry." Christine holds her breath, trying to force the tears down. She shakily places her teacup and saucer on the end table. This guy better be who he says he is. She can tell by his presence that he is.

"You lost three."

Christine doubles over and puts her head in her hands. "I lost three." Christine holds onto her head hard as if to keep it on. "I lost three." She grips her hair until it hurts.

The roaring fire and Nathan together are holding the space. She knows what this is. She's read all about it. She is grieving. It's natural. Animals do it. Everybody does it. Except her. Okay, so she's doing it now.

Nathan sits quietly in his chair. She is shocked how quickly the pain moves through her. Now it's good. Very good. Christine begins to nod. It's okay. Her breathing begins to equalize. It's going to be okay. She's okay. She sits back up.

Immediately chasing this relief is something else. Something far bigger. It's enormous. It wants out of her, but it's part of her. Oh fuck, it is going to kill her. She knows it.

She is beside her brother in the car. Her parents are up front.

She glances at Nathan. He is very still. Nathan is part of it. Everything that has happened is part of it.

Where the falcon had perched, her scalp tingles. Christine needs to get out of the chair. She lies down on the hardwood floor in front of the fire, on her side, looking into the flames. Her body takes over. Not just her body. Something more, in and out of her body, is breathing her, cleansing her of the shame, terror, hatred, and suffering. It's very thorough. She's hot, very hot, like her whole body is a hot coal.

Nathan moves his chair so that he's almost out of her field of vision. He's keeping watch. She gives him an apologetic glance.

"Don't worry," he says. "We're built for this."

"For what?"

"To heal."

THE BANK'S HARD, vinyl wingback chair makes Seth's back ache. He got here right after they opened and chose the one with the least amount of head grease. There are few materials that can take the kind of cleaning required to cut through human filth.

The hospital taught him that. He's happy he's stayed out of that place as long as he has. He's not going back. Forget that. No bloody way.

He's thought about medically assisted dying. It's legal now. He doesn't need anyone's assistance in that department. He knows how to die, thanks.

Seth is not afraid of pain. Although the pain is getting brutal, and he can't do the gym any more. It's not fair to the guys. They don't need to be worrying about geriatric Kassman while they're trying to lift. No one wants to look at his pathetic shrinking muscles.

Seth has been forced to wait almost two weeks to withdraw his own money. Now he's waiting some more in this waiting area. How much of his life has he spent waiting? He notices the plexiglass they installed around teller stations in the pandemic have remained and wonders how long the janitorial staff will bother to clean them.

He only wishes the pandemic had taken out more people. Not all the old people—that was terrible—just more idiots. Couldn't the good scientists have bred that into the virus? The idiot factor? No, it seems they aren't able to do that just yet. Well, maybe they did. You pretty much are an idiot if you can't simply stay two metres away from other people. Or understand the concept of a mask.

Seth has already done the mountain of paperwork about this withdrawal. Phone calls back and forth. Seth has been as patient as a dying man can be, and Dwight has been patient as a greedy bastard can be. Seth could actually hear Dwight licking his lips over the phone. Disgusting.

"Mr. Kassman?" Finally. A young girl in her early twenties approaches. Her little pink suit matches top and bottom. She looks deliciously clean. Her little pink nails sparkle.

He's already waited forty-five minutes. He makes himself stay calm. He can't get kicked out of the bank. He needs the cash. Today is the big day.

Her name tag informs him that she is called Ashli. What's wrong with y? Now he has to get up and follow her to another no doubt uncomfortable chair. He sits down where she indicates, at her desk. His diaper is riding wrong. He can't adjust it. Not here. It might freak out little Ashli.

The desk area is within earshot of the tellers and their growing line of people. The ceiling must be forty feet high. A whole lot of empty space doing nothing towers over him. Their money hard at work. The chair under him has seen better days. Metal arms and a black, woven cushion top that acts like Velcro and hangs onto everything. Seth can see hair stuck into the raised edge around the seat. This is disgusting. One of the hairs is short and curly. If he weren't in such a rush he'd ask for another chair.

"So, how can we help you today?"

"I'm here to … I'm here to process a large withdrawal I arranged for online—and over the phone."

"Right."

Ashli asks for his bank card and two pieces of government-issued photo ID. Her head bobs slightly back and forth as she types something in on her keyboard. She seems very professional. She probably had to have that size of a withdrawal approved by her manager. That's probably what the wait was about. It won't be long now.

"Um, Mr. Kassman, this is an awfully large withdrawal you are requesting."

"It's not a request. I set it up quite some time ago." Four people look over. Seth needs to soften his tone.

"Yes, I see the request here. The system has flagged it." Ashli's voice asserts that she is well trained in not giving people what they want.

"I wonder why? I know the money is there." He speaks more softly. He feels the concerned onlookers relax.

"It's not that. It is here, Mr. Kassman."

Seth is notified that the litre of coffee he drank while waiting for the bank to open wants out. There's nothing he can do to stop it. There it goes. He feels much more relaxed now.

This is what his whole life has bought him. Seth is going to enjoy this. He knows what to say, and says it. "I understand, Ashli. I have lots of time. Let's just work together to see what we can do."

Ashli smiles gratefully. Seth leans back into his chair and lets his young banking professional do her thing. Taxes, oh no, taxes! Wait, Seth will be dead before next tax season. Too bad. Sure, let's sign ten more forms. Seth uses his own pen.

Ashli launches into her educational discourse about liquifying assets right around the time Seth voids his rancid bowels. His guts never really recovered after his last round of chemo.

Seth knows the load he has just dumped far exceeds the capacity rating for this diaper. Especially after the coffee. He also knows that Ashli is trying not to react to the smell, but she's failing. Her little cupid face is pale.

Seth waits patiently. His waste has leaked past the diaper edges and soaks into the seat underneath him. He imagines the short, curly hair curling even tighter and shrinking away from the seepage.

He produces his old gym bag for the cash when the time finally arrives. "Does this work, Ashli?" It sure does. Ashli deftly sweeps up the bag and takes it to the vault at the back. Seth looks over at the teller line. He counts eight people holding their nose. One guy has his suit up over his nose. Like Count Dracula.

Seth sits in his still slightly warm seat and savours this moment. Live every day like it's your last.

"Mr. Kassman?"

There she is. Ashli is moving at full speed across the rug in her heels with his nine hundred grand. Her eyes are watering.

"Thank you so much for choosing us to do your banking with, Mr. Kassman."

"Oh, it was my pleasure, Ashli."

INGRID HAS TO TELL Mr. Worthington four times that Norman and she are having a private visit today. She's just managed to take off her underwear before Mr. Worthington tries once again to join them. She catches the door as it opens. "Mr. Worthington, don't worry. It's a special visit today, okay?"

"I want to see you too, Ingrid."

"You will. We won't be long and I'll make sure to tell you the minute we are finished, all right?"

She closes the door. You can't even lock the washroom door in this place. She wraps her citrus towel—from the South of France, it was—around herself. She has kept the beach towel they got on their honeymoon with its now faded pattern of lemons and limes. She bought it in the shop downstairs from their hotel suite, which, she has to admit, they rarely left, no matter the temptations out on the Promenade des Anglais. She retucks it around herself.

"Remember this, Norman?" She does a slow pirouette with the thin towel wrapped around her.

He gazes at her blankly. His once big frame looks diminished in the bed. She lets the towel drop to the floor and saunters over to him. She picks up one of his hands and places it on her bare breast.

"Norman, it's me. It's Ingrid. Your lover. Your wife. I love you, Norman."

He blinks rapidly and looks more closely at her with his nice hazel eyes. In a glimmer, it's gone again. But that is fine. Just fine. It was worth all the effort of doing this.

"Okay, Mr. Dee, time for—"

She doesn't manage to snatch the towel up quite quickly enough before Ariana the care aide has the door open.

"I'm so sorry!"

Norman looks over at Ingrid and laughs. Ingrid has not heard him laugh in a long while.

Neither has Ariana. "What's going on in here you two, hmm? May I come in? It's medication time, but I can come back."

Norman likes this care aide very much. She is so bubbly and kind. "Come on in, Ariana, we're just finished."

Ariana comes in and hands Norman his pills and a glass of water. Ingrid gathers her clothing and changes in Norman's bathroom. Ingrid pulls her top on just as Mr. Worthington pokes his head in with a big smile. He's forgotten his teeth. "Special visit today, Norman. Lucky man!" He then can be heard telling someone out in the hall what a lucky man Norman is.

Norman pushes himself up in his bed, getting frustrated. He reaches for the bar hanging over his bed and tries to swing his legs out at the same time. Ingrid watches as Ariana ducks his wildly waving arms. She is very tiny. Norman has always been strapping and hasn't begun to waste away too much. Ariana frowns and gives Ingrid a look as she goes out the door.

It's time to go. "See you tomorrow, Norman. We have something to look forward now, wouldn't you say, dear?" He gives her hand a squeeze. This too hasn't occurred in a long time.

Ingrid is smiling and a little dazed as she walks past the reception desk. Ariana gives her an awkward wave.

"Mrs. Dee, is that the first time you were doing that?"

"Yes. Did you see the change in him?" Ingrid sees that Ariana's brow is furrowed. She's never seen Ariana look so serious.

Ariana nods. "I did, Mrs. Dee." She rubs her earlobe nervously. "It's just … Do you think this is a good idea? Getting him all worked up? You know, in that way?"

"He knew me. He laughed, did you hear?"

"Yes, but—"

Ingrid looks at this little tiny woman who takes such good care of Norman. She comes from a country halfway around the globe to take care of Ingrid's ailing husband. Likely she has her own parents to look after there. Half of Ariana's money probably goes back home.

During the pandemic, Ariana was locked into this home for over a month. Ingrid cannot imagine what that was like for everyone. Norman hadn't noticed much, it seemed, by the time Ingrid was allowed back in. Norman's comfort was because of the kindness and bravery of people like Ariana.

"Really, Ariana. It was very special. I'll bet he recognizes you too. You are very important to Norman, you know. I can tell that he loves you. We both love you."

Ariana's eyes light up, and she gives Ingrid a little hug. "I love both of you too." She pulls back. "Okay. It'll be our secret."

TOM HAS LIED TO RON about where he is going. Tom is going to prison, to visit Shawna. She's awaiting trial, and no bail has been set.

The hospital's got her on video. All of it. The charges are many. The trial won't start until all the deaths since Shawna's rehire are looked at. The media is having a field day with it.

Tom is enjoying driving his brand new Volvo. It is the world's least sexy ride. Doesn't matter. It has the highest safety rating. The road follows the ocean out to the prison.

He wonders if the incarcerated women get to look at the ocean. Why is he wondering this? He's always thinking about fucked up women. He is wound around the axle of why these ladies do what they do. He needs to stop thinking about fucked up women. They made their choices, and that's why they're in there. They can save themselves. He pats the file sitting beside him in the passenger seat. He knows what he is doing.

Tom parks. This prison seems nice. It's weird how in Canada they put their prisons in the nicest spots. Manicured lawns, little clusters of trees, and this one has an ocean view. He hasn't done time, but he's no stranger to these places. He used to go and visit his friends, his homeboys. He's never been to a lady prison before.

Tom goes through all the screening and signatures. He watches as his pen, wallet, car keys, and file are x-rayed. After a series of buzzers as he passes through several doors, Tom finally gets to the meeting room.

There is a large window with a view of the ocean. The guards stand behind glass on the far side of the room. Shawna is sitting at a cement picnic table in grey joggers. He hardly recognizes her. Her long hair is cut off at the shoulders, and her face is without makeup. One leg is bouncing up and down as she folds and refolds a paper napkin. She looks like a scared little girl. But that scared little girl tried to kill a patient in her care. To kill Christine.

"Hey." Shawna doesn't get up to greet him.

"Thanks for seeing me," Tom says.

"Yeah, okay. I just didn't think you would want to. You know, after everything." She shrugs and ducks her head.

Tom sits down. "How long do we have?"

"I don't know. Do I look like I work here?" Shawna crosses her arms.

She is not going to intimidate him. "Okay, so I have an idea."

Now Shawna looks completely blank. "What?"

"I'm asking for custody of Terrine."

Shawna's eyebrows shoot up. "What? No."

"No? Are you sure?"

"No! Why in the world would I do something like that? Terry's parents have her."

"That's right, Shawna. And guess what else?"

"What, Tom? Tell me, Tom." Imitating his tone.

"They're too old, and they don't want her."

"Yeah, so?"

Her face is slack. She's probably high. What's with him and these punishing women? What is up with that? He's done with the cruelty. Done. No more heart-eating women. Just stay calm. He just wants to be a dad. That's why he's here. Get on with it.

"Do you really want Terrine to be with them? What about your parents, Mr. and Mrs. Meth Lab? Is that better? Is that what you want for your daughter?" The media's exposé of Shawna included a photo of her parents beside a photo of the wrecked house where

ALL IS WELL

their meth lab exploded, killing four people—but not them. The headline read, "Murder Runs in the Family."

"It won't be long. I'm getting out."

"You're getting out?"

"Yeah." She starts swinging her legs under the seat. Like a kid.

"When?"

"After the trial. Or like, during it. You know. When I'm liberated. When I'm vindicated. I shouldn't even be in here yet." There is a familiar look on Shawna's face now. She's looking at him like he's stupid.

"Is that what your lawyer is telling you?"

"That's what I know."

"The hospital has you on video, Shawna. All of it."

Shawna lets out a sigh and hangs her head. She peers up at him. "Family services would never let you."

Tom opens the file on the concrete table.

"Actually, I have been one of their youth-at-risk volunteers for the last five years. I'm a certified counsellor. They *will* let me." He turns the file around toward Shawna.

"All the inspections and interviews have been completed. I've been an emergency care residence for them for the last two years. I just had to upgrade my vehicle for full on adoption, which I did yesterday."

Slack Face is staring at him with her mouth hanging open. Tom slides his pen over to her. He looks over his shoulder at the guards watching them. They tap on the glass and motion to wrap things up.

Shawna slowly picks up the pen. "I know … I know what you must think of me." Shawna begins to sign at every red finger sticky Tom has meticulously placed on the document. "But I did right by Terrine. I never hit her, I never let Terry use in front of her, and we didn't smoke around her. I fed her the best food. You know?"

Tom puts his hand over Shawna's free hand, as the other hand signs the papers. "I know. But this—what you are doing right now, Shawna—this is the right thing for her."

Tom quickly removes his hand and waves at the glass. "Officer, will you witness this for us? I was told that—" He is interrupted by a buzz as one of doors opens. A woman built like a refrigerator does a stiff saunter toward them. He recognizes her from night class. Cheri. She looks very different in her uniform.

"I never meant to kill that bitch Christine," Shawna insists. "I just wanted to know where Terry was." She's almost smirking now. "She needed a smackdown. That fucking cunt."

He just has to endure a little more of this. Just let her talk.

"I just wanted to rock her world, you know? Ever want do that, Tom?"

Cheri the Guard arrives at the picnic table. Each boot comes down hard as she comes to a halt beside them. Shawna ignores her and leans back. "Now she knows. She's not fucking untouchable."

Here she is in grey, prison-issue jogging pants, a queen surveying her domain.

"I mean, who the fuck does she think she is?"

Tom isn't sure if it's the weak fluorescents, but Shawna's eyes are darker than he's ever seen them.

"All holy and shit. Yeah, right."

Tom looks at Cheri. He is relieved Cheri is close.

"Need a witness for some forms? I'll do you one better." Cheri winks at him and flourishes a notary stamp and an ink pad. "Nice stickies," she says, stamping and signing through the document, making Tom a father.

Tom glances into the rear-view mirror as the prison disappears behind him. He likes how the Volvo handles the winding roads.

He also likes how Cheri really pounded the stamp. So official. So dramatic. In the back seat is a four-hundred-dollar car seat. Soon his daughter Theresa will be sitting in it.

"I'M SO VERY SORRY, baby. Poor, sweet baby." Seth pats the dash of his beloved truck. He'll clean it when he gets home. He dials Dwight on the hands-free.

"I'll be by in an hour. Hey, are you there, Dwight? Can you hear me?" He's yelling. The traffic is loud.

"No can do. I have to arrange the armoured car."

"Don't tell me no can do, Dwight. I have the money, as we agreed."

"Show me."

"What do you mean? You want me to come over? Is that what you mean? I can be right there. No inconvenience or anything." Just my life's purpose that fat fuck is sitting on. No can do. Who says that? Losers. Losers like Dwight say that.

"Just take a picture and send it. Then I'll call the truck."

Seth hangs up, pulls over, opens the gym bag, snaps a pic of the cash, and sends it to Dwight. Traffic speeds by. People are oh so busy again. Seth doesn't feel well at all. He cracks a window. He's nauseated.

Most people slowed down for the pandemic, got a little nervous, watched the numbers rise on their news apps. Swapped conspiracy theories. Oohed and aahed during the civil unrest. Now things are zippy again. Zip-zip-zip. He won't be joining them. His zip is gone. Now he's sitting in his own filth and getting it on his truck. It's that fucking cunt Wright's fault. But now she's about to get knocked off her perch.

His whole body is cramping. He's dying, and his death is not going to be quick. He could barely carry the money out of the bank. He's breathing hard just sitting here. He probably should have filled out the suicide forms. He didn't think it was the right thing to do at the time. He didn't want to speed up what time he had left. Why do these fucking speeders get to live?

Seth's phone dings. It's Dwight. There's a big thumbs up. "Come right after close."

Seth fires up his baby. If he had done the medically assisted dying thing, he wouldn't be doing this now. He is supposed to be doing this. Nine hundred thousand dollars later. With every fibre of his being, he needs this. He's supposed to sort her out. It's obvious. Seth pulls into traffic and floors it. These fuckers won't be passing him any more.

After Seth cleans up and has a rest, it is finally time to pick up the evidence that will sort that woman out. He pulls up outside of Priceless Memories, and this time Seth just walks right to the back of the store. The door makes its bong-bong fanfare, the sound of justice finally coming down. One of the weird dusty dolls is pointing right at him. The doll is hot. Sexy. Big tits. Long hair. That's right. I'm the man. I'm the hero.

In the back of the shop, he finds Dwight cleaning the black candlestick.

"Stop! Put that down! I said to leave them as is. You better not have—" Seth drops the bag of money and rips the stick out of Dwight's paws.

"Whoa! I just thought, for the money—"

Dwight had worked in the middle. Thank you, Jesus! The fingerprints are still there.

"You have the money. I need plastic bags."

"What kind of bags?"

"Big ones. With ziplock."

"What?"

Seth looks at this big, dumb, mouth-breathing thief with raw contempt. "Did I say something confusing? Large ziplock bags. Let's go, Dwight."

Dwight shuffles over to the fridge and bends over. Seth is treated to a hairy ass crack and a grunt.

"Found some?"

"Can't use them."

Seth pushes Dwight aside to see a bunch of uneaten lunches.

"Why not?"

"Those are my lunches."

"Well, you're obviously not eating them anyway. Especially your veggies, Dwight." Seth dumps the food on the floor. He sees the medals poking out from under a rag and grabs them. "I'll consider these on the house."

"You didn't pay for those."

"Neither did you."

Sitting in his nice clean truck, he thinks about the service he's on his way to at Wright's church. It's perfect. The RCMP can wait until the morning. Seth wants to catch Wright and accuse her in front of her people, like in one of those British detective shows. He's already planning what he'll say. He has now run about three red lights. Safely, of course. But the elation of what is about to happen is almost too much.

He's never felt more alive. He looked up her services on the website. It's All Souls, November 2, so she's having a sunset service at five p.m.

Goddammit he's parched—he hasn't had anything to eat or drink all day. But he won't be pissing his pants in front of that creep show.

IT'S ALL SOULS DAY, and also the opening of their Room of Reconciliation. It's in the matching circular tower opposite the font, just where everyone enters the church and can't miss it. Larry built beautiful glass and wood display cases that wrap along the inside edge of the curved wall.

Christine walks past all the displays one final time before unlocking the heavy front doors. She pauses at the small oak table carved during World War II, with the original drawing of Mrs. Dee's window framed and sitting on top of it.

She glances up and sees James, Jackie, and the choir getting settled in the choir loft. She unlocks the door. There are already about twenty people waiting outside. Christine welcomes them and makes her way back to the office. She passes her new honorary priests and her new deacon, Andrew, as they head toward the Room of Reconciliation to answer any questions.

Andrew helps an old lady to her favourite pew, while an honorary helps a homeless man they have been getting to know to find a place where he won't feel trapped. Another honorary is verifying how to pronounce a name on the prayer list. She can hear people responding to the Room of Reconciliation as she makes her way up the nave.

As she gets closer to the office, she can hear Theresa laughing on the other side of the door. Ron must be there. Ron is Theresa's godfather and loves babysitting. Ron has biological grandchildren, but his family cut him off when he was deep in his addiction. No access to children or grandchildren—his swath of destruction was too deep. Ron will take her home to Tom's and put her to bed and wait for Tom to get back.

Christine enters the office, and Ron gets up. "Okay, you religious types, I'll be seeing you later. What are you doing tonight, praying for the dead?"

"That's right, Ron. Praying for the dead," Tom says.

"Sounds like a great way to spend an evening." Ron has provided Tom a lengthy list of people to pray for, but he prefers to stay away, to focus on little Theresa. One of the names was a young sponsee who overdosed just two weeks ago.

"Me and Theresa will watch some cartoons! And Grandpa will eat pizza!"

After Ron leaves, Tom and Christine have a small moment before the rest of the clergy and servers come into the office from out front. The others join them. They pray. The acolytes have lit the candles. The thurifer has stoked the thurible. They enter the church and process in silence. They arrive into the sanctuary and face the altar. The choir begins a haunting Kyrie. Christine turns to face a congregation of over two hundred. All eyes lift toward her as she raises her arms for the opening collect.

THE CANDLESTICKS *jostle slightly in the back of a king's cab. They are being carried swiftly toward a mission of justice in a powerful vehicle. A powerful Dodge Ram.*

This dying man is making use of them for justice. Or is it they that are making use of him? In all times. In all places. The play between dark and light gives expression here in this limited world to the limitless, to an all-embracing agreement, and to the stillness of infinity.

This is indeed a first. How is it that these forged symbols of unity have themselves been treated thus? The dying man takes a corner far too quickly. They bounce about in the box he's placed them in so tenderly, wrapped in a plush towel in this cab of a king.

Knowing all the laws of physics in addition to the laws that break the laws of physics, it is their estimation that the cab is far too high. This driver has purposefully extended the cab to this height for some value that some would call vanity. Others might call it insecurity, foolishness, or perhaps compensation for some lack in him. For some, all is vanity.

They have held their good company through the ages. They have witnessed the Black Death, inquisitions, burnings, beheadings, the Crusades, genocides. Although this man is not under such bondage, the suffering of this dying man is immense. His anguish knows no bounds.

May he have peace. The peace that passes all understanding.

Oh Holy Mother, Father, Keeper, Guard, Pain Bearer, Refuge, and Rock! Pour your Holy Spirit down. Make us instruments of your peace we beg of you! We ask this in the name of your Son.

AMEN.

CHRISTINE SHOULD BE exhausted but finds herself full of a buoyant energy after the service went so well, not a word out of place, every part of the liturgy flowing through her. She's doing the work she's supposed to do.

And what's more, she's going out on a date. With Nathan. This is a first. Mrs. Wilson noticed him at the Thanksgiving parish supper and eagerly informed Christine that he's the best friend of one of her cousins twice removed, and does she know how much he donates to the homeless shelter? "He's a good boy, despite all that wealth. Hasn't ruined him like it does."

All the congregants are gone, and only Mrs. Wilson, Mrs. Dee, and Tom have remained behind. They are enjoying a cup of tea together. Christine looks at her watch. It's almost seven. She's got an hour until Nathan picks her up.

He stayed all day with her on Thanksgiving. Helped with the setup and teardown of the supper, and then asked her out.

Christine has never been asked out before. She's nervous. Frances sent her a dress after their emergency trip to the hospital. A real dress, with an invitation to a ribbon-cutting of her Sterling Refuge for mothers and babies, a refuge she's set up in an old building she just happens to own downtown. There was a note: "There are other ways to mother."

That's where she and Nathan are going.

Mrs. Dee altered the dress for her, and it's hanging up. Christine steps behind the changing screen and puts it on. She looks at herself in the mirror. After the clearing that happened on Thanksgiving, she looks different. Her eyes have some light in them, and her face looks ... well, relaxed. She can sort of stand to look at that face now. That face will do. She can live with it.

Christine is about to put on her heels when she hears the back door open and feels a cold gust of wind enter. It must be a server who forgot their phone. Christine steps out from behind the curtain to find that MP, standing in her office.

He does not look good. His breathing is laboured, and he is sweating profusely. He is leaning on her desk with one hand. Grasped in his other hand is a ziplock bag holding the candlestick Christine whacked Terry with.

Tom stands up and offers him his chair in the semicircle of chairs by her desk.

With great care, the MP puts the blackened stick on the desk, and then shuffles around behind the desk and sits down in Christine's chair. He folds his hands on the desk.

The MP speaks. "Everyone sit down. Including you, Wright. I have important information." He clears his throat. "Important information to share with you all."

"That's the candlestick that got ruined on Easter," Tom says.

"I am well aware of that. Just let me do the talking, would you?"

Christine sits down. They all listen as he tells the story of Christine killing Terry with the candlestick. He points to the fingerprints. He points to the blood.

He draws the words out. "You will see, with magnification, that the evidence is all there."

Tipping his head back, he cites the eyewitness account that put Terry here that Friday evening. With a smirk, he apologizes for his state and explains that he is terminally ill, with not much longer to live.

Christine watches all this land on Mrs. Wilson, Mrs. Dee, and

Tom. Tom is sitting quietly but keeps nervously looking over at Christine. Mrs. Wilson is hanging on every word. Mrs. Dee harrumphs, like she knew this all along.

When he is finished, Mrs. Wilson actually raises her hand to ask a question.

"Yes?"

"Pardon me, Mr ..."

"I'm retired Warrant Officer Kassman."

Mrs. Wilson looks puzzled. "Warrant Officer Kassman, I mean, you would know far better than I, but don't you need a body? A body for a conviction of murder?"

The MP shifts slightly in Christine's office chair.

"Well, I can most assuredly help him out there. I know where the body is," Mrs. Dee offers.

"You do?" A look of what can only be called joyful anticipation appears on the man's face.

"Yes, it's right outside. I'll show you. But young man, let me get you a drink first. You seem to need one."

Mrs. Dee shoots to her feet so suddenly that everyone flinches. Mrs. Wilson is next to throw herself to her feet. "Yes, let us get you something to drink."

"Mrs. Wilson, I believe our officer looks like he would benefit from something served cold? Perhaps that iced tea we always keep on hand?"

Mrs. Wilson nods and leaves through the back door. Christine doesn't know about any iced tea. Always on hand? They don't keep it in here—the little fridge has a small milk in it. She's never seen iced tea anywhere. Not once during the sweltering summer was she offered iced tea, as she sweated through layers of polyester. Besides, it's November.

She can't believe Mrs. Dee knows where Terry is and is handing her over. Actually, she can believe it. She knew this was always the plan. Why would things be any different? She knew God was just toying with her, seeing how much she could take before she shattered. So Christine is curious now too. How much *can* she take?

Mrs. Wilson is back as quickly as she left. She places a mug on the desk for the MP. First iced tea and now a mug. He is getting extra-special treatment because he's so shaky and so visibly ill. And because he's finally going to take Christine off their hands.

The MP gratefully downs the mug's entire contents.

"Okay, let's get at that body, shall we?"

"Tom? Do you mind shining a flashlight for us? We don't want anyone to trip," Mrs. Dee says.

Tom looks at Christine, and she gives him a resigned shrug and points to the big flashlight by the door.

"I'll stay here. Don't worry. I won't run. I'm not even wearing shoes." After they leave, Christine sits down in her chair behind her desk and looks at the candlestick. There's a little piece of broccoli in the bag. The stick is too big for the bag and is poking out the top. How could there be fingerprints on that thing? Well, no doubt it's possible, but what isn't is this date with Nathan. That's just a little joke God is playing on her. She is finally going where she belongs. Locked up. Locked away.

She can hear them outside and see the flash of the light through the window. Yup, must be at the grave now. Mrs. Dee must be delighted. Finally getting rid of the troublesome Reverend. Christine wonders about the food in prison. Do they really have those trays with all the ridges? Probably only in the movies. Joey will be happy. There will be ample opportunity for interpenetration going on inside the Big House. Might get kind of rough. Violent fusions of all sorts. Maybe she'll be roomies with Shawna. They can become prison bffs. Try to kill each other every day, every night. Fun times.

Tom interrupts this reverie. He's carrying a piece of velvety cardboard with medals pinned to it. What is Tom doing with medals? He puts the medals and the matching candlestick from the set down on the desk. She looks up at him confused.

"They're asking for you outside," he says gently.

There will be handcuffs. He'll read her her rights, and she will be pushed into a waiting vehicle. She will receive assistance— the handcuffed always seem to require assistance in getting into vehicles. Courtesy for the condemned.

Christine goes out the door. It is All Souls. The dead have been prayed for. And tonight Terry will have more than prayers—he will have justice.

The frost is just beginning to form. Christine can feel it melt under her bare feet. Most of the trees have shed their leaves. Like this, the trees are imposing, commanding. Their presence is like a jury.

Her steps become intentional—they are leading her somewhere important. She stands taller. This is where she has always been headed.

There are no flashing red and blues. Just Tom's white flashlight trained on Terry's grave.

On top of Terry's grave lies Seth Kassman. Eyes closed, he is facing up to the night sky. Tom, Mrs. Wilson, and Mrs. Dee stand together in a small, silent circle around a very relaxed MP.

Christine begins to feel an itch around her heart. On the surface of her skin. Almost stinging. Like red ants. She looks down. Is she standing on a nest? She draws up the hem of her dress and looks at her ankles. Nothing there. Just frosty ecograss. The silence grows and deepens.

"What was in that iced tea?" she asks, a little flutter of hope starting up somewhere under her warming skin.

"Exactly what this fellow needed." Mrs. Dee is solemnly looking down at the MP.

"A clean and fast end," Mrs. Wilson follows up.

"Did ... did ... did you guys actually kill someone for me?" Christine squeaks like a little girl, standing there in her grown-up dress.

"Kill is not the right word," Mrs. Wilson offers. "I would say—"

"Please do me the service of not calling me a guy," Mrs. Dee says primly. "Do I look like a man?"

"What Ingrid is trying to say, Christine ..." Mrs. Wilson places a hand on each of Mrs. Dee's shoulders from behind.

The warmth is enveloping her now. Coming from all sides and making her downright toasty.

"Do try to let me speak. I can speak for myself." Mrs. Dee gives her cashmere cardigan a sharp tug. She looks around at all of them. "Well, I feel confident in speaking for all of us when I say that we saw a friend in a spot of trouble and thought she might need some help."

Christine's eyes widen. Her heart is pounding. "I can't believe this ... How, did you—"

Mrs. Dee furrows her brow, confused. "Poison ... as a matter of fact. Poison, my dear."

Mrs. Wilson purses her lips. "No different than medically assisted dying. This poor tormented soul ..."

"It's a little different." Tom scratches his head.

"Right, Tom, I had a peek at the assisted death concoction and I would say ours is far superior."

"No, I mean we didn't exactly assist him, did we ladies? By giving him that tea. That wasn't an assist. That was something else."

"I suppose you're right, Tom." Mrs. Wilson nods slowly in agreement. "More of a community-assisted death. We didn't have to burden the medical system. Gave them a break."

"They need that."

"They do!"

"After all they've been through."

"And it's not over!"

"No, right you are, it's not over."

Christine interrupts the frontline worker venerations. "No, I mean how did you know?" She keeps glancing from face to face, expecting an answer.

"Between the three of us, we don't miss much," Mrs. Dee says.

"Wow. This is a new feeling for me. Totally."

"Well, that's nice. Do keep in mind, however, that we need to focus now, Reverend."

Christine cannot believe how good her body feels. Not just her body. Her everything. Amazing.

Suddenly, Christine wants to show Mrs. Dee and Mrs. Wilson the finer points of shooting with the light pink Beretta. She also has the urge to dance. She can see Mrs. Wilson being a deadly shot. Mrs. Dee would appreciate the silencer. She can see herself dancing. Swooping through the labyrinth with her hair streaming out behind her. This is what it must feel like to be the Sunday school teacher, Ananda.

"Right. Right you are, Mrs. Dee. I'll pray for his soul."

"Well, that's fine. But then we'll lay Terrence Devonshire and Seth Kassman to rest properly. Right?" Mrs. Wilson insists.

"Right, Dominique, and then we'll return the Garden of Eden rug to where it belongs. After a good cleaning, of course."

Christine looks at Seth's face. It is completely peaceful. "This is ... I don't know what to say." Christine still can't believe this.

"You aren't invisible, you know, Reverend." Mrs. Wilson nods to Tom. He picks up the spade and hands it to her.

"I would stay and help you dig, but I'm getting rid of his truck. That's my part in the deal. The deal with these ladies. It'll be untraceable when I'm done with it."

"Tom, that's illegal. I can't ask that of you. You just got Theresa."

"It's okay, Christine. It's for a friend. It's for family."

Christine begins to bawl. Mrs. Dee rolls her eyes. Mrs. Wilson purses her lips. Tom opens his arms and beckons for the ladies to join in a group hug.

"Bring it in, bring it in, ladies."

"You don't belong in jail. You belong here with us."

Yes, this is what it's like to belong. All shall be well, all shall be well, and all manner of thing shall be well. She feels like singing. She won't, but she feels like it.

ACKNOWLEDGEMENTS

I would like to thank Stacey Kondla and Elizabeth Philips and all the great people at The Rights Factory and Thistledown Press. Also, I am so grateful for the family support in getting me to the When Words Collide Literary Festival, where Edward Willett, James Alan Gardner, Leanne Shirtliffe, Randy McCharles, and Jim Jackson heard the first few pages and encouraged me. Lastly, I would like to pay respect to Julian of Norwich and all the mystics who somehow, despite some challenges, share their visions.

KATHERINE WALKER was born and raised in Calgary, located in the Treaty 7 region on the traditional territories of the Blackfoot Confederacy (Siksika, Kainai, Piikani), the Tsuut'ina, the Îyâxe Nakoda Nations, and the Métis Nation (Region 3). She studied fine arts and design and after working as a graphic designer up north, Katherine joined the Royal Canadian Navy, which took her to the west and east coasts and out to sea. Her recent graduate studies in divinity, along with her artistic and military background, enhance her journey through life. You can talk with Katherine about divine guidance, dismantling underwater mines, or the connection between beauty and truth. Katherine is grateful for the tradition of story, the wilderness, and every breath in this amazing life. *All Is Well* is her first novel.